Hope you enjoy it, Kelsey, and happy holidays!

VCRepetto

December, 2013

V.C. REPETTO

Evernight Teen

www.evernightteen.com

V.C. REPETTO

DEDICATION

For my family, animal and human alike.

V.C. REPETTO

THE TEARINGS

V.C. Repetto

Copyright © 2013

Chapter One

The guy sitting at the next table coughed. It was an ugly, wet sound that made me look up from the exam sheet in front of me.

Fabulous. Last thing I needed was to get sick before the swim match.

He sniffed and wiped his nose with his stiff, already less-than-fresh sleeve, then lowered his hand back to his pencil and paper. Too bad for the person who'd have to pick that particular test sheet up.

Okay, back to the nonsense that would decide if I passed sophomore year or if I had to have "loser" tattooed to my forehead.

Sighing, I looked at the word problem. It was a geometry question, one of those that made no real sense except in the wonky world of math, and I'd already read it through at least three times. It still sounded like gibberish.

I glanced up at the rest of the sophomores, all bent over their own papers. Even Lisa, a row ahead of me, looked like she was trying to disarm an atomic bomb.

Standardized tests on a Friday morning, when all anyone could think of was being free to drool on our pillows until Saturday afternoon, at the earliest, was an interesting form of torture.

I glanced down my Scantron. I hadn't bubbled in a B for a while.

Ms. Cadiz's voice rang in my head, admonishing about the horrors of guessing, about the complicated fractions of point subtractions. Whatever. If I left it blank, I might forget and bubble everything wrong.

Without another thought, I shadowed in B and moved on to the next wordy nightmare.

* * * *

"How was it?"

I grabbed my gym bag from my locker. "Evil. That's how it was."

"Yeah, there were some questions I left blank," Lisa said.

"I just hope I passed. My mom will have a stroke if I don't." Slinging the bag over my shoulder, I leaned against the cool locker door, feeling the aluminum like a sheet of ice against my back.

"Well, she did try to get you that tutor."

"I don't think anything would have prepared me for some of those questions. I'm pretty sure I got the test that was in Russian or something."

She smiled. "You can tell your mom that. I'm sure she'll believe it."

"No, but I really was distracted. There was a guy coughing up a hairball next to me."

"Ew!"

"It's probably whatever is going around the school, the flu, or something, but I don't want to even think of getting sick." I grabbed Lisa's arm and started to lead the two of us to the gym. There was a large crowd of students still exiting the cafeteria where we'd had the exam, each one with varying levels of fear sketched on their faces.

"You can still swim if you're sick."

"Not at a state championship. Mr. Grason will never let me even get on the bus."

"It was just a kid coughing, will you stop worrying? You'll be fine."

I arched an eyebrow at her. "You're a fortune teller now?"

"No, I just know you have paranoid tendencies."

I laughed and pulled the gym door open. "I hope you're right. Otherwise I'm coughing all over your lunch tray."

"You're so gross," she muttered, following me into the sweet and tangy smell of the school gym.

"If I can't go to the match, you can't, either."

* * * *

Mom was waiting at the kitchen table when I finally made it home enveloped in a chlorinated cloud. It was so much the norm for me that I barely smelled it anymore, but I knew it could curl unprepared noses.

There were so many questions on her face and she was tugging on her shirt like she did when she was about to leap out of her skin.

"It was fine," I said, before she exploded with anxiety.

"Do you think you passed? No, I don't know if I want to know. If you're held up a year, then you'll have trouble getting scholarships and—"

"Mom, chill. Geez, I love the faith you have in me."

"Maya, you and I both know math is not your forte."

"Okay, but it's not like, kryptonite or something."

Mom sighed and stood. "I know I'm exaggerating, but I want you to do well."

I smiled. I really should have been used to this by now. After all, it would always been just the two of us, a household of semi-insane females.

"There's eggplant lasagna in the oven; it'll be ready in a few minutes."

"Yum. It's completely vegetarian?"

"Yes, Maya. I was really tempted to get the beef one, though, and pass it off as meat-free."

"Mom!"

"I didn't. This one is the nice, boring vegetable variety."

Putting my back-pack and gym bag down, grabbed two placemats, and dropped them on the kitchen table. It was a rickety, ancient thing that was small enough for us to have to squeeze our glasses in between our plates. We'd tried eating at in dining room, but it felt strange in there, with so much space around us we actually lost the salt shaker once. Actually lost it in the tablecloth dunes.

Okay, Mom wasn't the only one who had a penchant for exaggeration.

"How was work?"

"Oh, it was glorious. Norman was out sick so the office was so quiet! He really should be sick more often."

I snorted. "As a social worker, aren't you supposed to have, like, compassion for your fellow human beings? You can't just walk around wishing people sick."

"Norman's a pain."

Laughing, I set the rest of the table.

"Actually, there's something going around, I think." Her face tightened. "Are you taking your vitamin C tablets? Your Echinacea?"

"Yes, Mom. I'm taking them all. You'll probably find me one of these days sprawled on the floor, yellow and dead from a vitamin C overdose."

"It keeps you healthy. We also should get your flu shot one of these days before the season starts."

I shook my head. "It's tested on animals."

"It is not."

"Yeah, it is. I'm not getting the shot."

Mom rolled her eyes at me and plopped a serving of lasagna onto my plate. "You can be a real pain sometimes."

"Oh, like Norman. One of these days you'll be wishing I get sick so you don't have to put up with me anymore."

"Yup, that's exactly right. Seventeen years with you is quite enough."

I gasped in mock horror and flung a dinner roll at her, hitting her square on her forehead. My aim was definitely improving.

* * * *

Monday rolled around and with it, the swim match.

The rain had started the night before and continued, flooding the school parking lot and making the ten of us, the half-asleep swim team, groan as our uniforms started to sag.

"I wasn't planning on getting wet this early," Lisa said as we climbed up the bus steps.

"Yeah, I already have a cold," Trevor said with a sniff. "I'll probably die in the water. Float right up to the top like a fish."

"You're sick? Does Coach Grason know?"

"Do you think I'm stupid? Of course he doesn't know. And you better not tell him."

I lowered my bag onto one of the fake leather seats. "I'm not going to say anything, but if you throw up in the pool..."

I grimaced as I sat down, hearing the seat's wet squelch. Somehow, the rain had found its way inside.

"At least this pool's one of those warm ones." Rachael, the team captain, extended her legs along the aisle in a stretch.

"Yeah, the last one was so cold I thought they'd have to use an ice pick to get me out."

"Which one was the last one?" Lisa asked.

"The one in Jackson High," I said.

"Right. No, but this one is supposed to be one of those super fancy ones. I mean, it should be, from how annoying their swim team is. You'd think they trained in a gold-rimmed pool."

Trevor laughed. The sound twisted into a hard cough that hurt my throat just from hearing it. "Do you want an aspirin?"

He shook his head. "I've already had four this morning." He wiped his nose and leaned against the seat. Was it just the light, or were his cheeks flushed?

"Maybe it's not a great for you to compete today. You're not looking your best."

"I'm fine. I just need, like, the largest cup of coffee on Earth."

Lisa shrugged. "You'll have to wait until we get back for that."

Trevor nodded and closed his eyes. I watched him for a few more seconds, then sat back to wait for the bus to finally get going.

V.C. REPETTO

Chapter Two

We were getting pummeled by the other team. They'd beaten us in every race but one, the one Rachael had swum, and we'd only won that one because the other girl had gotten a leg cramp halfway through.

I'd already done my race, losing by an arm's length, and was sitting at the bench, fantasizing about the tea I'd get when I made it home. A gallon of it, with enough lemon to pucker my whole face.

Coach Grason was sitting a few feet down the bench, his shoulders slumped, his whistle dangling like a dead snake from his neck. He'd started the match in his usual way, with lots of teeth-grinding screams and pounding of fists into any surface available. But slowly, as one by one the races dropped away without wins, he'd shut up and slunk to the bench. We'd be screamed into next year when we got back to school. Not that that would help much now.

There were two more races, Trevor's and Cheryl's, and then we could head back home, preferably never to see these people again.

I sighed and leaned forward on the bench. I caught movement from the end closest to the pool. Lisa waved at me with a limp hand, and I waved back with just as much enthusiasm. I was turning away again when I saw her frown, her gaze flicking to the opposite side of the pool.

Following her eyes, I spotted Trevor. He was gripping the wall with one hand and his chest with the other, his nails digging into his own skin as if he wanted to tear it off his body. From my seat, I caught a flash of red, like a beacon across the room.

A sharp gasp cut through the splashing and dull murmuring as someone else caught sight of Trevor and his odd behavior.

Trevor wavered on his feet. The people around him were pulling away as they caught sight of his face, suddenly as pale as the wall behind him.

"Hey," I murmured. My voice was stuck to my throat and I had to clear it to be heard. "Hey, something's wrong with Trevor."

Lisa was already on her feet, hurrying towards him.

"Mr. Grason," I called out. I couldn't tear my eyes away from my teammate, who was sinking to the floor. A harsh screech tore from his mouth, as his hands darkened with his own blood.

I wanted to run for help, to scream for someone to call an ambulance, but I couldn't unglue my hands from my sides or my legs from the tiled floor. Instead, I only watched as people, like a wave, first receded in horror then surged forward again, crowding around Trevor so that I couldn't see anything anymore.

That shook my paralysis. I ran to our coach, who was only now becoming aware that there was something wrong at the opposite corner.

As I reached him, a horrible gurgling filled the room, coming from the boy now on the floor.

"An ambulance!" someone screamed. "We need one, now!"

I patted my sides, but I'd left my phone in my gym bag in one of the lockers. Mr. Grason had his out already and was running towards Trevor with fear carved into every inch of his face.

There was a scream from someone in the crowd surrounding him. I shivered at the sound, so guttural and dripping with fear.

"What's going on?" Rachael asked, trotting up next to me.

"I don't know."

"Everyone! Step away from him, give him space!" The other team's coach yelled over the commotion as he tried to herd the growing crowd out of the way.

I tried to spot Trevor, but he was invisible in the mob of students.

Coach Grason came up to us. "Rachael, gather our group and get them back to the bus." He handed her the attendance list, although with only ten of us, it was wholly unnecessary. "Make sure everyone is on that bus. I'm going to stay here to wait for the ambulance."

"Of course, Coach."

Without another word, he turned and headed for the crowd.

"Can you help me?" Rachael said.

"Yeah, sure."

The majority of our team was still on the benches, all wide eyed. I knew the questions they had, because I had them too: he'd been sick, but had he been *this* sick? What exactly did he have? And the worst, most uncompassionate one, could we catch it?

"Lisa, Rick, come on, we have to get back on the bus."

"No, but Trevor—"

"The coach is going to stay with him. Come on, guys."

Slowly, Rachael and I gathered the swim team by the exit door. I stood on the tips of my toes to catch

17

Coach Grason's attention, giving him a quick nod when he finally looked my way. He nodded back and waved us out.

* * * *

Trevor wasn't in school the next day, or the days after that. We bombarded our Coach with questions, but either he didn't know much more than we did or he had one flawless poker face.

I even called Trevor's house three times, since his cell was disconnected or out of batteries, each time letting the phone ring until the machine picked up. Each time, I left a quick message, but no one called me back. If I'd known his parents' office numbers, I would have called them as well.

Even the rest of the school was talking about it for the first couple of days, coming up with the nuttiest suggestions: everything from a werewolf transformation to a parasite that tried to eat its way out like in *Alien*.

But like everything that didn't have an immediate effect on us, we pushed the whole thing aside after two weeks. Math tests and history essays took precedence, grabbing and keeping our attention.

A month passed before the next incident.

I was balancing on my stool in the chemistry lab, completely focused on the slide in front of me, when a scream ripped through the room's silence.

A slide crashed to the floor and shattered behind me.

"What the hell was that?" Jennifer, my partner, squeaked.

Our teacher was already up and leaving the room. "Stay in your seats. I'll be right back."

Like that was going to happen. Within seconds of him exiting the classroom, everyone was spread around, whispering.

I kept my mouth shut and edged towards the door. Two teachers and a custodian hurried past it, taking the right corner towards the Social Studies wing.

The intercom suddenly clicked.

"Teachers, please keep your students in their current classrooms. No one is to leave. We are in a lockdown."

A lockdown? We'd never had one of those before, not even a rehearsal for one.

The murmuring grew louder.

"Do you think there's someone in the school?" asked Lacy.

"Maybe, like a shooter."

"Carl, stop saying stuff like that; you don't know what you're talking about," I said.

He lifted his eyebrows. "You don't either. Why do you assume I'm not right?"

"Just stop it. We'll find out later."

"Yeah, sure we will."

About that, at least, Carl was right. No one told us anything, not even when we were allowed out to the buses and hastily gathered car-pools. It was noon, and we were already being released for the day. This was odd enough to let us know something bad had happened. Lisa and I met by our lockers as teachers ushered us out the door.

"Did you hear it?" I asked.

"Yeah. It was awful."

I grabbed her arm to keep from being jostled apart. "Did your teacher tell you anything?"

"No, but I don't think she knows. She wasn't one of the ones who ran to find out what happened."

"Mine was, but he's not answering any questions we asked him."

I saw Rachael pushing her way towards us in a way that would have made her a good candidate for the school's football team.

"Rach, you okay?' I asked.

"It was Samantha Fellone."

"What was?"

"The one they took away."

Lisa grabbed her arm. "Wait. Who's they and why did they take Samantha?"

Rachael blinked at the two of us. "You don't know what happened?"

Lisa and I shook our heads in unison.

"Okay, come on." Grabbing both of us by the arm, she pulled us towards the school entrance and out into biting winter air. "Let's get away from the teachers so we can talk."

As she pulled us toward the student parking lot, Lisa paused. "I'm going to miss my bus, though."

"I'll drive you home," Rachael said.

We followed her to her car, a serviceable if not entirely clean Mazda.

It was only when the three of us were sitting, with me leaning forward in the backseat to catch every word, that Rachael started to talk.

"I was going to the bathroom, the one in the Social Studies corner, and I heard someone groaning. There were a few things I imagined, all of them things that could get people suspended, so I stopped by the bathroom door, trying to make up my mind if I should go in or not. That's when I heard another voice. I didn't recognize it, but she was asking the person groaning if she was all right and stuff like that. She kept asking, but the other girl didn't answer. I went in then, and saw a girl knocking on a closed bathroom stall. A strange gurgling sound started, like someone was gargling with, like, mouthwash. The other girl got curious enough to step onto the toilet on the next stall and look in. And then she started screaming."

Rachael stopped and looked at the two of us.

"You heard it, I'm sure."

We nodded.

"Okay, I'm not proud of this next part, but it's too late now to do anything about it. I actually left the bathroom. I didn't want to know what she'd seen in the stall, and I definitely didn't want to be there when teachers ran in to check what was wrong. So I waited around the corner. Ms. Alonzo and Dr. Spielman ran in first and dragged the girl who'd screamed out. Ms. Alonzo took her away. Then Mr. Reed came into the girl's bathroom and ran back out seconds later already on his cell phone. He said Samantha's name, that's why I know who she was. A minute later, the principal declared the lockdown, so I had to run back to class."

Lisa and I looked at each other. "But what happened to Samantha?"

"She's probably in the hospital."

"No," I said. "I mean what happened to her in the bathroom?"

Rachael shrugged.

We sat in silence for a moment, each drawing up blood-filled scenarios that would have deserved the lockdown and the early release from school. Maybe she was another case of teen pregnancy gone worse than usual. But Samantha didn't seem like the type of girl who'd get into that kind of trouble. Or perhaps she'd been assaulted and had run into the bathroom. How injured would she have to have been, though, to make another girl scream just from the sight of her?

"What if something like what happened with Trevor happened to Samantha?" Lisa's voice was thin and much softer than usual.

Rachael frowned. "But we don't even know what happened to him."

"Exactly," Lisa said. "No one's told us anything about him and I'll bet no one will tell us about Samantha, either."

"I don't know," I said hesitantly. "I don't want to start any kind of gossip."

Rachael gasped. "Gossip? Us?"

I hit her lightly on the arm. "You know what I mean. Let's just wait until tomorrow and see if any of the teachers know what happened."

"Oh, I'm sure they know," Lisa said. "The question is if they'll be willing to share."

* * * *

I waved goodbye to Rachael and opened the front door of my house. A clatter of dishes made me freeze in surprise. Mom's car hadn't been in the driveway. As I inched farther inside the house to investigate, the sharp smell of something burning tugged at my nose.

"Maya?"

I sighed. It was just Derek, Mom's boyfriend. I followed the trail of smoke to the kitchen, where he stood, peering down into an actual recipe book.

"You scared the shit out of me," I said. "Where did you park your car?"

"In the side entrance. Didn't your mom tell you I was coming over?"

I thought back to earlier that morning. She might have mentioned it, but I tended to block out anything that started with his name, or even anything that rhymed with it. I hadn't stayed fully conscious through any sentence with the word "ferret" in it for years. Not that there were many of those.

"No. I don't think she did. How did you get in?"

"I have a key."

Now this was news. And not welcomed news, either. "Oh."

Derek looked up and cocked his head. "It's not like I'm going to steal anything, Maya."

"I didn't say you were." I grabbed a banana from the fridge and threw my backpack on the nearest chair.

He looked back down at his book. "I wanted to surprise Jenna with dinner, but it's not looking too good. Any ideas?"

I peered into the pan, which had a hunk of unrecognizable, charred meat that was slowly sticking to the bottom. "I think it's way past done."

"Really?"

"Oh, yeah." I peeled the banana and grabbed my bag again. "You do know I'm vegetarian, right?"

I left the room without giving him a chance to say anything else.

Being completely honest, I didn't know why Derek left such a sour taste in my mouth every time I saw him. There was nothing plainly wrong with him, no aggressiveness or drinking issues; he wasn't domineering or patronizing; he even kept sarcasm for the rarest, most unavoidable moments.

At first, I thought it was a momentary dislike I'd grow out of, like my dislike of broccoli. I imagined he thought the same thing. He waited me out, patiently staying out of my way through the first few months, being, now that I thought about it, extremely forgiving to every sharp word I had for him. Which were many.

But as a year passed, then another, we both realized this wasn't going to get much better. I'd gotten older and could therefore fake my way through conversations better, but the fact remained: Derek was just not someone I liked.

Mom had noticed from the moment he'd stepped through the door that first night two years ago. She'd known my reaction before even I did.

She used to chide me for every unkind thing I said about him, but by now, she'd given up on the whole thing. She liked him, and that was enough. After years of being alone, taking care of me without anyone else's help, that should have been wonderful.

I wanted to respect that, to be proud she could hold her own even against my opinions, but I failed miserably. She was my mother and I wished she'd like someone *I* liked as well.

Pathetic, yeah.

Okay, the whole story was that it really had been just the two of us from the moment I was born, since my biological father had ridden off into the sunset without my mom. I had his name but nothing else. And none of the curiosity to go looking for more. So, yes, jealousy might have played into it the teensiest bit. That was something I couldn't blame Derek for. That was my own little bit of lunacy.

* * * *

The dinner was as awful as it'd looked. The steak, which I didn't try, was so dry they'd needed to get the big, barbeque steak knives to manage. The vegetables Derek had thrown together at the last minute for me were by turns rubbery and gooey. A marvel how he'd managed to do both.

I ate a few bites, enough so that I wouldn't get into too much trouble with mom, then pushed the plate aside.

"We had to be dismissed from school early today."

Mom's eyebrows lifted, though if it was in response to the mouthful she was chewing or my words, I didn't know.

"What happened?"

I told them the whole story, including everything Rachael had seen. Their faces got tighter and tighter with each word.

"We think it might be sort of the same thing Trevor had."

"Who's Trevor?" asked Derek.

"A boy on Maya's swim team."

"He freaked out the other day at our match and started to tear at his skin. He was bleeding all over the tiles."

Derek was unusually quiet. I'd expected all sorts of questions. He was, after all, a pediatrician.

We sat in silence a few seconds before Derek cleared his throat. "I'm going to tell you both something, but you *cannot* repeat it. To anyone." He looked up, going first to mom and then to me. He held my gaze, the knowledge of our mutual issues rippling beneath the surface.

I shrugged. "Okay."

"Seriously, Maya. I could lose my job over this."

I sighed. "I promise."

He clenched the fork in his hand. "A little kid came into the office two days ago with his mother. He was having trouble breathing and had a little bit of fever, but it looked like just the flu. About ten minutes into the consultation, he started grabbing at his chest, like he couldn't get a breath. He stopped after a bit, but he wasn't acting right."

A chill ran down my back.

"I gave him a sedative and called an ambulance to take him to the hospital for tests." He paused. "When I called later to ask about him, no one remembered him at all. They refused to tell me if any doctor had even looked at him. I tried calling his mother but got no answer."

Mom sat back. "It could just be an oversight. You, of all people, know what a mess hospitals are."

Derek shook his head. "Something about this doesn't feel right." He turned to me. "What happened to Trevor?"

"I…well, an ambulance came and took him away."

"Is he back in school?"

"No. He's probably still getting better."

"But you don't know for sure."

"No, but where else would he be?"

"And his parents?"

I frowned. Now that I thought about all this in light of what Derek had shared, it did strike me as odd. "They haven't answered their phones, either."

"And now this new case."

Mom pulled at her shirt, that little habit that made me nervous as well. "There has to be a reason for all this. No doubt, we're being really dramatic over something stupid."

Derek and I looked at each other.

"I hope so," he said, though he didn't sound in the least convinced.

That sentiment had to be the only thing we'd ever agreed on, ever.

V.C. REPETTO

Chapter Three

Friday had finally come again and I couldn't stop looking at the clock. I shouldn't have been; I was being ridiculous. It was just a movie with Lisa…and her brother.

I'd tried on three different outfits and had almost dragged my mom into the whole process before deciding that the blue dress looked better against my cinnamon hair. Biting my lip, and therefore smudging off some of the lip-gloss, I sat down on one of the kitchen chairs to wait.

Finally, the bell rang and I forced myself to walk to it.

"Ooh, you look nice," Lisa said as soon as she saw me.

"Thanks, so do you."

She gave me a wink and moved aside.

Martin had a large, wide smile on his face. I could feel my cheeks reddening as I moved aside so he could come into the house.

It wasn't so much that he was good looking. He was. But there was an aura about him, like he had a miniature sun glowing inside him. It was impossible to be in a bad mood when he was around.

The strong jaw and gray eyes didn't hurt, either.

Lisa, who couldn't see her brother as anything other than the kid who used to put mud patties in her bed, wagged her eyebrows at me. At least this time Martin was looking away.

"We should get going or we'll be late," he said.

The three of us piled into Martin's small car; Lisa had jumped immediately into the back seat, leaving me to take the passenger's. I wanted both to strangle her and to give her a kiss. But, of course, this would now mean I had to make actual conversation with her brother.

"So, uh, how's school?" I asked.

"Boring. Probably the same as in yours."

Martin was a year older, and he went to a military academy nearby. He'd started out at our school but switched after freshman year. That had resulted in much groaning from the female population.

And that seemed to be it for me and my conversational skills. One question and I was fried. This always happened. Later, I'd come up with a million different things I could have said, all wittier than the last, but for now I could have been thumped on the head, and it would have rang as hollow as a log.

"I heard this movie is good," Lisa said.

"Yeah," I agreed.

"Yeah," Martin repeated. "At least there'll be lots of action."

It was probably one of the most awkward car rides I'd ever had anywhere, and that included the time I'd thrown up on a teacher's lap during a bus ride in fifth grade.

But finally we parked and headed for the theater's entrance.

The smell of butter and salt dragged us forward to the concession stand. Although I didn't think I could eat much, I bought a bag of gummy bears.

Martin smiled. "I love those."

"You can have some if you want."

"Great, thanks."

Lisa tried to control her laughter at my epic awkwardness. At least we weren't there to watch anything overly romantic. Just some action movie to which I barely knew the name.

In a maneuver worthy of Olympic recognition, Lisa managed to seat her brother and me together, while she took a seat on my other side. I'd have to kill her after the movie.

"So, how's school?" Even as I said it, I realized I'd already asked him that. Lisa snorted into her Pepsi.

Martin smiled and cleared his throat. "You kind of already asked me that."

I laughed a little too loudly. "Yeah. If you haven't noticed by now, I'm a bit of a moron when I'm nervous."

"Nervous? Why are you nervous?" His eyes stayed on the screen in front of us, where a movie trivia question blinked.

Great. Now what the hell did I answer?

Next to me, Lisa was almost choking on her malt balls.

"No reason, I'm just a…nervous person by nature." So, so lame.

"Oh. Must be tough to be you, then."

"Oh, yeah. It is," I mumbled and stuffed my mouth full of gummy bears to keep from saying anything else.

I thanked all the angels in heaven and anywhere else when the lights finally dimmed and the previews began. In the dark, at least, I could blush at my idiocy as much as I wanted.

We were about an hour into the movie and I'd managed to finally relax a bit when a man in the row closest to the screen stood up with a groan. There was a bit of shuffling as people waited for him to sit down again, but he didn't. He stood, weaving a little from side to side, just a silhouette against the flash of a car chase on the screen in front of him.

"Hey, sit down!" someone called out from behind us.

"We can't see anything."

"Sit, man!"

But the man just continued to stand there, without even turning his face towards us.

Next to me, Martin leaned forward in his seat. "I think there's something wrong."

A large woman lumbered down to the man's row. "Didn't you hear us? We can't see if you stand up like that." She stepped closer, confrontation written plainly across her face. Suddenly, she froze.

"Someone get help." Her tone had changed from argumentative to frightened.

"What?" another man called out, tone laced with agitation.

"This guy's bleeding."

She stepped away, never taking her eyes off him, and headed for the theater's exit.

At her words, my eyes widened in the dark. It was too much of a coincidence to believe this could be happening once again without the incidents being related. I shot a nervous glance towards Lisa.

In seconds a theater employee came into the room with a large flashlight.

"Sir?" He touched the man's arm. "Sir?"

There was a ripping sound, like someone tearing a piece of paper out of a notebook, followed by a shriek, and the theater employee dropped the flashlight with a metallic clang.

"Shit," he said, retreating.

Two teens ran down to the first row as if they planned to help the sick man. One look was all it took to send them screaming.

"Oh my God, he ripped his skin off!"

"Fuck, he has no skin left!"

Lisa and I looked at each other. The fear in her eyes was bright enough to be seen in the darkness.

"We need to get out of here before everyone panics," Martin said.

But it was too late. The floor vibrated with the feet that pounded through the aisles, everyone trying to get out at the same time through two narrow openings.

We were trapped in our row as people pushed one another to get to the green exit lights. The theater employee was trying to keep order, his voice rising to a shrill scream as no one took the least notice of him.

Martin grabbed my hand. If it'd been on any other day, at any other moment, this would have sent me blushing, but right now his rough grip frightened me into action. I took Lisa's hand in mine and squeezed.

With one shove that demonstrated his game winning football skills, Martin yanked us forward into the aisle, crashing into a couple of women who teetered on their heels. I only had time to turn around and make sure no one was trampling over them before someone smacked against me.

A nucleus of pain in my right side made me gasp.

"Maya?" Lisa called.

I nodded that I was fine, though I was still full of pain.

We made it somehow to the doors, and poured into the carpeted hall. People were still pushing from behind even though we were already out of the room, as if they couldn't get far enough from the man who was probably dying, if he wasn't dead already.

Martin dragged us to a corner sheltered by the bathroom's entrance.

"Do you think anyone called 9-1-1?" I asked.

Martin shook his head. "I don't know."

"That guy needs help."

"He's probably dead already, Maya. Didn't you see him?"

"No." I'd been too preoccupied with not ending up as meatloaf underneath the crowd's shoes to look his way too closely.

"Let's just go," Martin said.

"But the police might have questions," Lisa said.

"Well, they can ask someone else. Come on."

As much as I wanted to do the right thing and make sure the man inside was getting the help he needed, I also wanted to get as far away from the theater as possible. There was something unspeakably dangerous about what had happened tonight. I felt it in my blood.

"Fine." Nodding, I let Martin lead me outside.

I could only hope what I was feeling, the pulsing foreboding, was wrong.

* * * *

It wasn't.

Three more students at school had to be carried out on gurneys the following week, and two more, we heard, from a neighboring school.

All of them the same: complaint of flu-like symptoms with extremely high fevers, followed by the ripping of skin. That was the only point in which the cases varied. Some people attacked their chest cavities, others their faces or necks.

None of them came back to school.

The teachers skirted our questions as best they could, though I was sure it was more from their own ignorance about what was going on than from the need to keep us in the dark. They carried on with classes, ignoring the few vacant seats, but it was hard to miss the slight pause in their lectures when a student sneezed or coughed.

"More and more children are coming in with the same symptoms," Derek said one night after I mentioned yet another classmate who'd not shown up for a few days. "I don't know what to tell their parents, really, since antibiotics don't make much of a dent in the fever." He sighed. "And I'm not the only one at a loss. All my colleagues think this is something new. Something we haven't seen before."

"Is it contagious?" Mom asked.

"We don't know for sure, but it appears to be."

We'd had scares like this before, of course, with swine flu and bird flu, all frightening in their own right, but managed in an efficient manner. It was the complete silence from news-teams and government officials now that left me sleepless. Were these concentrated incidents or was the rest of the country experiencing them as well? I was sure it couldn't have spread past the US. There was no way the rest of the world knew anything about it. Of course not.

Mr. Grason called the team in a day after the latest victims were taken away. He looked like he hadn't slept an hour in days. Maybe the rumors were right and his wife really was sick.

"I know we have a few matches left this year, but because of whatever is going around the city, the school dean has told us we should cancel them. The other schools agree that until everything is resolved, we should avoid travelling."

Lisa, Rachael, and I looked at each other, as everyone else on the team frowned.

Rob, a senior, sat up. "What about Trevor, though? We haven't heard from him in like a month."

Mr. Grason looked down at his feet. "I don't know what's happening with Trevor. I've called his house and his parents' offices numerous times, but no one's answered or returned my calls. I don't know what to think. All we can do is try to keep the rest of us as healthy as possible." He wiped his forehead and refused to meet our eyes.

It wasn't much comfort, and he knew it.

The whisperings started soon enough, a veil of gossip woven around a few facts.

"I heard from my cousin that there are buses passing through picking up any homeless people they see," Rachael said during lunch.

"Yeah, I heard the same thing. Dad says the buses were painted black, and had boarded up windows."

"The one my mom saw," Carla, a freshman, said, "had huge spotlights on the roof. She didn't see them on, but I doubt anyone could hide from them."

"But is it true they're taking the homeless?" Lisa asked after yet another retelling of second-hand news.

"Well, have you seen them around?"

It was true. When I thought about it, I realized the usual spots where the homeless slept — in the park close to the school, in the corner between the church and the post office — had been empty. There were no cardboard boxes or piles of mismatched, soggy clothing. Even the sharp smell of wine and urine had almost disappeared from the walkways through those spots.

"What do they want them for?" I asked.

No one knew, not the teachers or our parents.

And the number of students getting sick increased. In February there'd been ten students who'd left with the usual symptoms; by the beginning of April, there were forty-five. Entire families disappeared, leaving behind jobs, friends, and homes.

"I've had two families, with their foster children, completely vanish," Mom said, slumping back on her chair. "I don't know what to do. No one has seen them in days."

"It's the same with many of the children I'm treating. All the ones I've sent to the hospital for tests have disappeared." He sighed, glancing up at me as if I was the one he needed to warn. "I really don't know what's going on, but I don't like it."

Even with all of these warnings, with everything that had been hinted at, we did as most of us tend to do when confronted with truth we don't want to face: we made a joke, or shook our heads, claiming we'd know soon enough. We reassured ourselves that if anything too serious was happening, the government would tell us. It would help us all find a solution.

We went on with our lives, ignoring the gaping holes where people use to be.

V.C. REPETTO

Chapter Four

The truth came trampling through our world the day of the annual book fair. As always, the fair was held in the downtown area where the public library and the community college shared a street. The tents for the different booths had been up for days already, with the banners marking each publishing company that would be there for the three-day event.

It was the only thing our city could really pride itself with. Each year, authors from all over the world would come to read excerpts of novels, poems, or whatever they were promoting and artisans of all kinds would flood the streets with their knitted handiwork or clay sculptures. It was one of the only times I was happy to live in this city.

"We'll be late, Mom," I said, tapping my fingernails on the car door.

"You know they start these things late. Always."

She dug out a few coins from her pocket for the parking meter, while I watched people walk down to the ticket booth.

One of my favorite authors was speaking in five minutes, and we still needed to walk two blocks to the assigned space he'd been given.

"A-ha. Another quarter. Jackpot." Mom stuffed it into the meter and brought out a wet wipe from her purse. We'd all started using them, along with hand sanitizer. So much so that just the smell of the wipes made my stomach twist into a knot.

"Can we go now?"

Lisa was supposed to meet us there and was probably wondering where we were. Although, since she did know my mom quite well, she'd probably suspected we'd be a few minutes late.

I hooked my arm around mom's purse, a habit I'd kept from the few trips to Disney we'd made when I was little, and we plunged into the loud, colorful crowd.

In the throng, it was impossible to believe there were people missing. It seemed absurd, like we'd made it up. I almost managed to convince myself of it.

We were crossing the street to the assigned spot for the reading, with seconds to spare, when the crowd in front of one of the coffee stalls rippled apart.

"Wait," I said, squeezing Mom's arm.

A woman was pushing her way to the front of the line, slamming right into the stall in her frantic hurry. From where we stood, I could see the top of her face, her swollen eyes as she turned from person to person.

"I think she's saying something."

I led the two of us closer, until the woman's voice reached us.

"Help! Please!" She leaned towards the crowd, her hands wringing together. She seemed unable to stop their shaking.

As one unit, the crowd backed away, allowing the space in the front to grow.

"Please, they're taking my son!"

Frowning, I looked around, past the crowd. Beyond the people shopping, there was as cluster of violent movement, pulling and dragging that clashed with the rest of the atmosphere.

"Mom!" I pointed at what I was slowly realizing were two men and a boy of no more than seven years. He was kicking out with his feet. He had on shoes with neon streaks on the sides, so that every time he moved, the light caught the shining fabric. And the men… I'd never seen anyone dressed like that outside of a science-fiction movie. They had dark shirts and pants, tight fabric that clung to their bodies. A dark surgeon's mask completed their outfits, covering the lower half of their faces.

I shivered.

"What are they doing?" Mom asked, pulling me closer to her without realizing it.

I shook my head. I had a suspicion, but it was so absurd, I couldn't bring myself to say it.

"They're taking him! I need help!" The mother's shrieks had grown louder and sharper, drawing the attention off the nearby activities. People stopped, gripping books tighter. Conversations trickling off as only the woman's voice rang out through the street.

"He's sick and they're taking him!"

"What is this?" someone asked. "What are you talking about?"

With a shaking hand, the woman pointed to her son and the men who had him. The crowd turned. There were some gasps followed by the rumble of questions.

The little boy had been immobilized now. One of the men had his small arms locked against the sides of his body while the other one had pushed the boy's hands behind his back. They had him lifted, parallel to the ground. I couldn't see the boy's face, but I could hear the soft whimpering that was coming from him.

"Hey," a man said from lower in the crowd. "What are you doing to him?"

"That is not your business," the man holding the boy's hands said.

"Put him down; you're hurting him."

The two men exchanged glances. The one at the boy's feet released his grip, allowing them to slam against the pavement. The child's chest rose and fell with difficulty, and his whimpering was turning bit by bit into groans.

The man strode towards the waiting crowd.

Mom's hand gripped me tighter.

"We have our orders." The voice boomed over us.

A woman near me raised her voice. "What orders?"

"That is not for me to share."

"He's my son!" the boy's mother screamed. "He's sick!"

"Precisely, ma'am."

With a nod of the uniformed man's head, two more men dressed in the same dark outfits stepped out from behind the stall and grabbed the woman.

I gasped. I hadn't even seen them approaching.

"Wait," the woman said. Her voice had lost its fight. "Where are you taking me?"

"With your son."

She nodded. All at once, the desperate woman who'd broken her way to the front of the crowd was gone, replaced by one who was nodding and smoothing out her shirt.

"Okay. If I can go with him, okay," she said. "Are we going to a hospital?"

But the men had stopped paying attention to her. They herded her to where her son was. The man still holding the boy released him enough for a quick embrace.

The people around us were already turning away with slight puffs of boredom. There'd been no real fighting, no ripped clothes, not even a splash of blood. Even Mom was breathing a bit easier.

I wanted to think everything was over, that it'd been a misunderstanding on the woman's part. There'd been no violence, right? They'd manhandled the boy a bit, but if he'd been kicking it was the only thing they could do. Right?

The words rang false in my head.

I turned and glanced back at the woman and her son. The men had separated them again, the two holding the boy drifting forward as his mother was pulled back. She kept stretching her neck to keep an eye on her son.

Just before the whole group disappeared around a corner, the woman looked back and found my eyes. The fear on her face took days to erase from my memory.

* * * *

I started waiting for the six o'clock news every afternoon. It was the only station to mention the strange flu those first few weeks, and although it hadn't spoken about it outright in a while, its news anchors did make oblique suggestions. Like telling us to carry hand sanitizer wherever we went, and suggesting we give up on kissing people on the cheeks for a while. Until "this all resolved itself".

"We should do something tonight," Lisa said one Friday in which two other students had been taken to the hospital.

Now, the teachers no longer waited for the later symptoms. Like the principal had suggested, a cough got you sent to the nurse's office, where, if you continued to cough or sneeze, you'd be picked up by one of the many new ambulances that had begun to appear throughout the city. They didn't look like the regular 9-1-1 ones. These were dark, with only a large, painted red cross on the front. Every time I saw it, I thought that it looked like the cross had been swallowed by night.

"Tonight's the speech," I said.

"Oh, that's right. Well, do you mind if I come over to your house to watch it? My parents are in one of their silent-treatment moments. I wish it were silent, though. It's more of a 'slamming-doors-and-muttering-under-their-breath' kind of treatment. It drives me nuts."

"I can imagine." Although, to be honest, I couldn't. I'd never heard my mom really fight with Derek. Sure, they'd had arguments, but it was easier, since he could just leave and go cool off at his own house.

So that night, Lisa, Mom, Derek, and I sat in front of the television, waiting for President Finster to march his way down to the podium where he'd be giving his speech.

"Do you think he'll tell us what's going on?" Lisa asked Derek. She, for some reason, thought he was a great choice for my mom. The only real fight I'd ever had with Lisa had been, incredibly enough, about my behavior towards Derek.

"I doubt he'll tell us the truth. He'll probably just give a vague few lines and call it a night. He's not going to want to scare us."

I frowned. "Just by giving this speech he's scaring us. He's making it serious by giving it this much attention."

He shrugged. "We'll have to see what he says."

Ten minutes later, after nodding to the vice president and to a few other members of Congress I couldn't identify, President Finster started speaking.

"Fellow citizens, I have asked for this conference tonight because I know the concern that is filling every one of your homes. Like you, I have been carefully watching the developments of the illness that has been affecting some of our cities. Now, I want to reassure you that these incidences are concentrated to a few parts of the country. We are not dealing with an epidemic or anything close to it."

There was a hiss from somewhere in the audience, which brought the President to a stop.

"Wow," Mom said. "That's a first."

President Finster cleared his throat. "We are not in any danger, I assure you. The affected cities are few, and the situation is not at a critical level, but there are a few things we, all of us, can do to keep ourselves and our loved ones safe. Some of these many of you are already doing, for which I applaud you and encourage you to continue. Simple things like washing your hands more often, carrying wipes, avoiding shaking hands. These things can be invaluable to quickly obliterate this flu. Despite what you might have heard, that is all this is. A flu that has become sturdier than what we are used to. It's no more than that."

This time a voice rose out of the crowd. "Liar!"

I leaned forward, frowning. This had never happened before, and it was more frightening than anything I'd heard throughout the past weeks.

The President flicked his eyes to his left, to someone off screen, then looked at the camera.

"Some of you have already seen the new ambulances that have been designed specifically for the patients who are suffering from this flu. In the next week or so, you will start seeing more of them, but I want to make clear that this is nothing to be afraid of. These ambulances are state-of-the-art, with all the newest technologies, and they are equipped to transport your ill loved ones to centers that will bring them back to full health."

"What is he talking about?" Derek said. His eyes were locked on the screen.

"We have top doctors and nurses who have been trained specifically to deal with this illness, and they will do their best to speed up the recovery of all our affected. Now..." He tapped his fingers on the podium and gave one of his famous, crooked smiles. "I urge you to cooperate with the officers and emergency personnel who have been assigned to help. It only makes things more difficult for them when we question their actions. I assure you all they have been trained extensively. They have our best interests at heart, so each of us has to be as helpful as possible. Together, I know we can put this behind us, but only if everyone cooperates and trusts in their government. In this, as in everything, we are stronger if united." He gave a small nod and stepped back. Applause filled the hall and commentators immediately started the recap.

Mom turned the TV off.

We sat in silence for a couple minutes, until the words I'd been holding back finally came out.

"I don't like this."

"Neither do I," said Derek. He had a deep frown in the creases of his forehead.

"What?" Lisa asked.

I shook my head. "I don't know. I can't pinpoint exactly what it is, but something feels wrong about what he just said. For one thing, how can we know for sure that this disease is just a version of the flu? We've seen it. It doesn't look like it."

"I'm sure the President knows more about it than we do," Mom said.

"And this whole thing with the centers… What centers is he talking about? I haven't heard anything about them."

"It makes sense, though," Lisa said. "It explains where all the kids who haven't come back to school are."

I looked at Derek, who had his eyes on his feet. He didn't meet my gaze.

"But some of them have been gone for weeks. We haven't heard anything from Trevor and his family in almost two months. That can't be normal."

"Maya, we don't know anything about this disease. It could take much longer than the regular flu to clear the system. I'm sure the doctors are making sure the people at the centers are completely cured before releasing them again." Mom cocked her head at me as she always did when she thought I was being too negative.

But so many words had been said that rang out of tune in my head. "Cooperate", President Finster had said, and "trust", but trust based on what, exactly? He hadn't really given us any facts.

I sat back as Mom guided the conversation to other topics. But as I smiled and nodded, even laughing as Lisa told one of her summer camp stories, I couldn't shake the unease that hung heavy like a quilt around me.

V.C. REPETTO

Chapter Five

With a swipe, I pulled the black mask off my face. "I can barely breathe with this thing."

"That's kind of the point. Then you can't breathe in any germs or whatever," Rachael said.

"Yeah, but you do realize I need oxygen to live, right?"

"Well, I think they make us look cool." Lisa narrowed her eyes over her own mask, trying to look mysterious but only managing an awkward squint.

I smiled.

Three days after the President had given his speech, every school and every workplace we knew of had given out these masks and enforced their use everywhere except inside our own homes. In school, if we were caught without them, we'd be suspended, which seemed just a teensy bit dramatic. The teachers had to wear them as well, but we had no idea what their punishment would be if caught without them. If someone from, say, outer space, peeked into one of the classrooms, they would have seen a bunch of bored, wannabe-ninja lookalikes.

I lifted my backpack higher on my shoulder, cursing my geometry teacher for giving us problems to solve out of the huge textbook. It was like she didn't even care some of us had to walk home.

That was another thing that had changed practically from one day to the next: the school buses had been stopped. We'd gotten official letters from the dean and governor telling us, in the kind of convoluted wording that forced the eye to immediately start skimming, that we'd have to find other ways of getting to and from school. It was all for our own health, of course. It was too much of a risk putting all of us in a cramped space like that. So instead, some of us had to get carpools together, or get bikes. Lisa and I had been counting on Rachael's car since she lived close to us, but it'd chosen this week to sputter, cough, and die in her driveway. Hence, the walking.

"A van picked up my neighbors last night," Rachael said.

I watched her bite her bottom lip.

"I didn't even know they were sick. They left everything behind. My dad saw the whole thing and they asked him to look after their dog. But he's forbidden us to step foot inside the house, or their yard, even."

"Maybe you can call animal services," Lisa said.

"Dad says they won't come to an infected house."

We walked in silence for a bit. I tried not to think about what would happen to that dog.

"Martin told me one of the vans took away two of his classmates yesterday," Lisa suddenly said.

I frowned. "But he's in the next city. Has it gotten that far, then?"

"Apparently. The school is being really strict about it, too. They make each student take their temperature once a day in the infirmary."

"That's insane," Rachael said.

"It sounds illegal, too," I said.

"No, they cleared it with whoever is in charge of those things."

"What does Martin say?" His name pulsed on my lips.

"He's for it. He says if that's the way to keep people safe, then it's a good thing. It's not such a big deal, really."

Rachael blinked. "You would have no trouble, then, getting your temperature taken every day at the nurse's office?'

Lisa shrugged.

"It's a complete invasion of privacy," I said.

"But it'll keep us safe, right?"

Rachael and I looked at each other, but decided not to say anything else. Maybe she was right. Maybe it was worth losing a few minor privacies for the good of the majority.

A rumble from behind us pulled me out of my thoughts.

"A van," Lisa said. "No, don't turn around." She grabbed my arm to keep me looking ahead. "Put your mask on, quickly!"

My fingers fumbled with the elastics that would keep it in place, and the mask dropped from my hands to the pavement.

As I knelt to pick it up, the van came to a stop. "Shit."

The passenger's door opened and a woman in uniform walked up to us. Well, to me, actually.

I grabbed the mask and stood again, trying to brush the dirt off the fabric with hands that had begun to shake.

"What is going on?" the woman asked. Her voice was muffled behind an even more dramatic mask made out of some kind of plastic. It glittered in the afternoon like a pool of black nail polish. The rest of her uniform was black as well, with not a single speck of color on it.

"She...well..." Rachael started.

"I was readjusting my mask and I dropped it. It won't happen again." I smoothly placed the mask over my head and back where it belonged.

The officer (she had that air of authority about her. Oh, and a gun) looked from me to Rachael and Lisa. "How long did you have your mask off?"

"A couple of seconds. No more than that."

"Do you know I could arrest you for this? You're endangering yourself and your friends by not wearing it."

"Yes, officer, I realize that. I am truly sorry. It was a mistake."

"What is your name?" She brought out a sleek phone.

"Maya Salaise."

She typed it into the phone.

I didn't dare look over at Rachael or Lisa, but I could feel their fear pushing against me.

"You seem to have no prior records. Nothing at all."

"No, ma'am."

She flicked her eyes back to me. "I'll let you off with a fine this time. But I will write it up and the next time you'll end up in jail. Do you understand?"

"Yes, ma'am. Thank you."

She brought out her pad and filled out a ticket, then handed it to me. Four hundred dollars, it read, although I had to blink a few times to believe what I was seeing. Mom was going kill me.

"You need to pay that by the end of the week or one of us will come pick you up." She looked at me one more time, then stomped back to the van.

I couldn't take my eyes off the paper in my hands.

What the hell was going on in this city?

* * * *

As I'd imagined, Mom almost had a stroke when she saw the fine. Color left her cheeks, accentuating her dark eyes as they strayed up and down the paper.

"I can't believe this," she whispered.

"I know, I'm sorry. I took the mask off for a couple of minutes walking home. If I'd known there was a fine and it was that high, I wouldn't have risked it."

Mom's head jerked up. "How could you have taken the mask off, Maya? With everything that's happening!"

She wasn't mad about the money, then.

"I didn't think it was such a big deal. It was just Lisa and Rachael walking with me, and neither of them is sick."

"You know they've told us to wear the masks everywhere. You have to do as they say. Do you want to catch whatever this thing is?"

I blinked and looked away. "No. Of course not." All I could think of, all I could question, was how we'd gotten to this point, how we'd gone from the speech the President had given telling us not to worry, to this moment when my mom was on the edge of panic at my taking off a mask? When had things changed so dramatically without any of us really noticing it?

* * * *

All those questions flew out of my head when I woke the next morning and swallowed.

My throat was raw, throbbing, and dry.

Panic rose immediately.

I was sick. I'd caught it.

I dug my nails into my hands and tried to get a hold of my galloping fear. Maybe I'd just slept with my mouth open during the night. That could be it, right? It didn't need to be the worst thing imaginable. Except, I knew it was.

In seconds I was bolting up out of bed and running to the mirror hanging from my closet door. It hurt to open my mouth. Patches of red and fuzzy white had spread across my tongue and palates, making me wince when I touched them.

Sudden tears made my vision waver. Whatever this super-flu was, I had it.

I brushed my tears away with violence. There was no time for that right now. I had to think. My first instinct was to run into Mom's room and tell her, but I made myself stand still for a few seconds more. Once she knew, she'd call the ambulances; there'd be no stopping her. They'd take us away to the health centers, so this might be the last few minutes I had to face this without needles poking at me.

As much as I tried to convince myself that allowing the ambulances to take me to the centers was a good thing, I couldn't stop my stomach from clenching at the thought of riding in those black monsters that patrolled the streets. I wanted to stay home.

On impulse, I grabbed my cell off my night table and pressed one of the speed dial buttons.

Derek picked up on the fourth ring. "Maya?"

"Hi."

"Is everything okay?"

I hesitated. This was it. Once I told someone, there'd be no stopping this. "I woke up with a sore throat."

The silence on the other end lasted for only a beat. "I want you to check your mouth in a mirror and—"

"I've already done that. I have red and white patches."

"Do you feel sick? Feverish?"

I thought about it. "No. I feel okay."

"That's good. A sore throat doesn't mean you have it."

"And the patches?"

"It…it varies." I heard the truth in his voice, though. The patches were not a good thing.

"What should I do?"

"Put your mask on and wait a few hours to see how it progresses. If you start coughing, call me back. Actually, call me back anyway."

"And Mom?"

"Hold off on telling her, just until we know for sure."

But we did know for sure. There was no way Derek could hide that from his words. His tone spoke volumes. He was just doing what he could to comfort me. I wouldn't have thought he'd be concerned about me. Although he really might be worrying about Mom.

"Okay, thanks, Derek," I said and hung up before he could say anything else.

Mom. I couldn't risk getting her sick.

Grabbing my mask (*would I have been okay if I hadn't taken it off yesterday?*), I put it over my nose and mouth and left my room.

I walked carefully past Mom's room and headed straight for the patio door. Although winter was still at large, the air was mild enough for me to be okay with one of the cardigans I'd hung by the door.

Out here, with my mask on, I couldn't be a danger to anyone until I decided what I needed to do.

I settled back on one of the patio chairs, wincing each time I swallowed at the fire that seemed to cling to the inside of my mouth. Despite my nerves and fear, drowsiness circled me, closing in by the minute until I was dangling on the edge of consciousness.

"Maya?"

My eyes opened. They were dry and itchy. Someone's head was leaning over me, their face darkened by the sun in the background.

"You okay?" It was Lisa. She shifted to the right and her face came into focus. Behind her, Martin was staring at me with eyes that were slowly narrowing.

That's when I noticed Lisa had no mask on. I pulled myself up from my slouch and made sure my mouth and nose were still covered.

"Hi. I was just sleeping."

"Yeah, we could see that," Lisa said, smiling.

The sun was so bright in my eyes, forcing me to look down at the dirt.

"Sorry for showing up like this without warning, but mom made some fresh scones and I thought you might want to come eat some with us. We were careful not to wake your mom."

I nodded. They'd come in through the fence door, as Lisa had always done when we were little and she had something so interesting to show me it couldn't wait for my mom to open the front door.

I realized Martin was still watching me, so I sat up even straighter and cleared my throat. Big mistake.

The pain shot through me and I couldn't stop the groan from coming out of my mouth.

"Lisa," Martin said. "Get away from her."

Lisa half-turned. "Huh?"

"Get away from her." He was standing very still, as if in the presence of a dangerous animal, which, I guessed, I sort of was.

"What are you talking about?"

"She's sick. She's got it."

Lisa's eyes flew to my face, looking for my laugh at her brother's melodrama, for anything that would tell her I was fine.

I said nothing, just closed my eyes.

"Oh, God." The grass crunched as she stepped backwards. "You'll...you'll be okay, Maya."

I kept my eyes closed, not wanting to see the fear on my friend's face. I focused on her words. I would be okay. I'd be fine. Of course I would.

"Come on, Lisa!" Martin hissed. The two of them retreated, from the sounds of it, right back out through the fence's door.

Only then, I opened my eyes and stood. I had to tell mom before the vans came, as I was sure now they would. Martin's voice, the fear in it, left no doubt about it.

As I walked inside, mom came out of her room.

"Hi, honey." Her smile was still crooked with sleep.

"Mom."

She looked up at me. It took her less than a breath to know something was wrong. Her eyes focused and the drowsiness fell off her at once.

Still, I had to say the words. "I'm sick."

Mom stepped forward. "What do you feel? When did it start?"

I told her everything, including what Derek had said.

"Let me see your mouth." She got even closer, and I took a few giant steps backward.

"You don't have your mask on. You'll get it, too."

She shook her head as if this were the most ridiculous thing I'd ever said. "It doesn't matter. Let me see."

"Mom—"

"I'll be fine. I'm not worried about me." She took my head in her warm hands, her skin still smelling like the moisturizer she used every night, and took my mask off. "Open your mouth."

I did as she said, as I'd done countless times throughout the years. In the past, mom would peek at the swelling or redness or whatever was bothering me and coo something comforting. Something that let me know everything was going to be fine.

She kept her face clear of expression as she stared at the white and red patches, but she couldn't come up with anything to say that would make me feel too much better.

"Who else knows about this?"

"Martin and Lisa came over a few minutes ago. They guessed it."

"Do you think they'll be calling the ambulances?"

I nodded.

"Okay." She rubbed her forehead with her hand. "Pack a small bag with essentials: underwear, your jeans, and a few shirts. I'll do the same. I'm sure the center will have you wear hospital robes, but just in case."

Both of us headed to our rooms, a certain calm having descended on us as we realized we'd have to leave and nothing could be done about it. Mom's certainty that the vans and the centers were a good thing spread to me as well. I wanted to believe it.

I dumped everything out of my backpack and stuffed it with clothes, and, at the last minute, the book I'd been reading yesterday.

I was pulling the zipper up when I heard the sirens. Despite every bit of logic I had, I still felt the stab of betrayal. Martin and Lisa had sold me out. Yes, they wanted to make sure I got help and no one else got sick, but they should have let my mom do it.

Pushing the hurt away, I stepped back out into the hall where Mom was waiting with one of our old beach bags slung over her shoulder and her mask covering her nose and mouth.

"Put yours back on, honey." She took my hand in hers as the sirens grew louder. And when the ambulance's doors slammed closed on our driveway, and I'd begun to tremble, she squeezed it hard, until all I could feel was her warmth.

V.C. REPETTO

Chapter Six

Two officers and a paramedic stood in front of us. They were dressed completely in black, of course, with only their foreheads and eyes showing out of their plastic masks.

"Maya Salaise?" One of the officers, a man, spoke.

"Yes," I said and stepped forward.

"Someone has reported that you are showing symptoms. Is this correct?"

"Yes."

"How long have you had them?"

"Just this morning."

"And you've not had contact with anyone else in that time?"

I thought of Lisa and Martin, but I'd been wearing the mask the whole time they'd been near me. "No."

"How did the person who reported you know you were ill, then?"

Shoot. "I...we spoke over the phone."

The man's eyes held my gaze for an instant, then looked over at Mom. "Have you experienced any symptoms?"

"No."

"Are there other members in the family?"

Mom was about to open her mouth when I jumped in. "No. It's just us." No point in dragging Derek into quarantine as well.

The man nodded and turned to the other officer. "As you know, ma'am, we'll be transporting you to one of the healing centers."

How many were there, exactly?

"There, your daughter will get the care she needs."

Mom nodded and walked forward, towards the ambulance. I followed.

"Keep your masks on at all times during the ride," the paramedic, a woman with a red cross stamped into her uniform, said.

It seemed strange that she'd not even bothered to take my temperature or any vital signs. But Mom had already hopped up onto the ambulance and the officers had disappeared around the front.

"Wait. We need to lock the door." I started to head back, but the paramedic grabbed my arm with one thickly gloved hand.

"We'll call one of your neighbors to do it later."

"Oh."

Her grip was strong and my arm was starting to hurt. Never releasing me, she led me inside the ambulance.

The door closed and locked behind me.

I frowned.

Inside, it looked like no ambulance I'd ever seen, although to be fair, I hadn't seen that many. There was a wooden bench on one side and that was about it.

"Aren't there supposed to be machines and things in here?" I asked Mom.

She was looking around, as if the equipment could be hiding somewhere around us. "Yeah. But I guess since they're taking people to the centers at the early stages of this flu, they don't need all of that."

"Okay, but a wooden bench? How about adding a cushion or something."

"It's to decrease germs, most likely."

We sat down just as the ambulance hummed on. At the first turn out of our street (which we guessed, since there were no windows where we were seated) both of us almost slid right off the bench.

"I'm sure it won't be a long ride," Mom said, holding on to my arm.

* * * *

But it was. Three hours long, with no breaks and no one even taking a peek to see if we were still there and hadn't fallen off somewhere around hour two.

By then, the pain in my throat was close to unbearable. Every swallow sent sharp, hot pins up and down, making me wince. A glass of water would have helped, or, even better, a cup of tea.

Mom had tried calling Derek with her cell phone to let him know what happened, but there was no reception. Same thing with my phone. That struck me as strange.

Finally, the ambulance slowed, then stopped.

"It's about time," I said.

"They probably wanted to get to the center as soon as possible, Maya."

There were doors slamming and footsteps nearing where we were. The door unlocked and opened.

Early afternoon light trickled in, cheerful after the cold, artificial one we'd been under for the past few hours.

"Come on," the male officer said from the doorway.

We eased out of the ambulance and looked around, expecting to see a tall building dressed in institutional gray, with people in scrubs and masks.

Instead, we saw what looked like an old bus terminal with at least two dozen school buses painted a

63

dull black with every window covered up with metallic blinds. The buses had large reflector lights on top of them.

And there were people. So many people.

"What is all this?" I asked.

"They're going to the centers as well," said the paramedic.

I gasped. All these people! The disease had spread much more than we'd thought.

"Let's go," the male officer said and waved us over to one group of about sixty people standing by one of the large buses.

There was nothing as orderly as a line, but we placed ourselves at the end of the crowd. A woman next to me gave a hacking cough right into her mask.

"Stay in this group. It'll take you to the right place," the female officer said. All three of them turned around, ready to leave.

"Wait," Mom said. "Don't we need some kind of intake notification?"

"Everything will be taken care of once you get to the center." Then they were gone.

There was a hiss of metal as one of the bus' doors opened and a man in the usual black uniform started herding people inside. On his shoulder was a rifle.

"Mom," I breathed, taking in the weapon's smooth shape. "There's something going on here." I looked around and saw men and women in black with the same type of rifles in their grips. A chill that had nothing to do with the illness ran down my back.

The people in front of us looked around as well, but gathered their bags and stepped up onto the bus without putting up any kind of struggle.

"I don't know if I want to go in there." I stepped backwards, thinking about nothing but getting away from the bus.

In moments, I had a rifle pressed to my head. "Inside," someone said from behind a metallic mask.

Mom gasped and lunged forward, but another officer grabbed her arms and pulled her up into the bus.

"Inside. Now."

"Okay," I muttered, my voice shaking so much I wasn't sure if they could understand me. I grabbed the handlebar and pulled myself up. A shove sent me through a second door that'd been installed past the driver's seat and into complete darkness.

The first thing that hit me was the smell.

A combination of sweat, urine, and something darker. Blood, perhaps. It was strong, unbearably strong, and my stomach twisted at the thought of spending time in here.

The noise was almost as bad. How many people were in here? I could even hear a baby crying somewhere on the opposite end.

Someone pushed into me from behind, slamming my backpack against my body.

"Where am I?" the person said, pushing into me again. I lost my balance and my arms flew out to grab onto something. They touched the bus' walls, which were wet as if they'd just been washed, but also slightly sticky. I steadied myself.

"Maya?" Mom's voice cried out from somewhere on my right. Her voice was sharp with fear.

"I'm here, Mom. Hold on." I grabbed the cell phone I'd put in my pants before leaving the house and touched one of the keys at random. A thin, sickly light surrounded me. It didn't illuminate more than a couple of feet in front of me, but it allowed Mom to push her way towards me. Her hand squeezed my arm.

"Are you okay?" she asked.

"Yeah, Mom, I'm fine." But we were still getting pushed by the people who were continuously pouring into the bus. Lights went off and on as people brought phones out, throwing light at our surroundings until a picture of where we were formed in my head. It was a bus, yes, but the seats had been removed. There were no aisles, just an open space getting packed with more and more people. The windows had no glass on them anymore, just the metal panels blocking light and air from us.

I looked up and saw a handrail about a foot above my head. To keep us from crashing into one another when the bus started, I supposed.

A rough, wet cough sounded from somewhere in front of me.

The full horror of what was happening finally collapsed onto me. This bus, packed with people who were either sick or who had loved ones who were sick, was going to take us to the centers like this. Standing up, with barely enough room to breathe.

"Mom, check your phone. Do you have reception?" We needed to get out of here. We couldn't allow them to take us to the centers like this.

My hands shook as I brought my phone out as well and tried to dial Derek. Nothing. I had no bars, no connection of any sort.

"Don't bother," said someone a few feet away.

I looked up to find a girl, probably a little older than I was, hugging a pillowcase that'd been filled with things to her chest. One hand had a firm hold on the bar above us.

"No one has reception. I've been trying it for two days."

"Wait, you've been in here two days?"I asked. "No way."

"Yeah."

"But they must stop for the night, right? We have somewhere to sleep?" Mom asked.

The girl, who I could now see had a sheen of sweat on her forehead, snorted. "Yeah, sure. It's the Ritz every night."

The door slammed behind us, making some people shriek, and a few more cough.

"I'd grab on tight, if I were you," the girl said.

Mom and I reached for the bars. What would happen to the people in the middle, though, the ones who weren't near the bars?

I found out as soon as the bus moved a minute later. There were screams as people shifted, hitting themselves against everyone around them. Shouts and moans started to fill the dark bus, crowned by a baby's frantic screech.

"I don't understand," Mom muttered.

Like the majority of us, I kept hitting my phone's keys to be able to see around me. At one corner, illuminated by someone else's phone, I spotted a little boy propped up against the wall by bags. His mouth was gaping, his eyes open and flicking violently from one place to another.

"He's almost dead," the girl next to us said. "His fever's so high he doesn't recognize his mother anymore."

"But why isn't he being given anything? Do the officers know?" Mom asked.

"Of course they know. They don't care. His mom gave him some aspirin to see if it'd help, but he's just gotten worse."

It made no sense. The officers were just going to let this child die, without doing anything, not one thing to help?

His mother, the woman standing above him, wouldn't take her eyes off him, not even when someone crashed into her and made her bang her head on the metal bar.

"I'm Christina, by the way," the girl said.

"Maya, and this is my mom, Jenna."

"Are you sick?" I asked.

She nodded. "Since I live alone, I didn't drag anyone else into this mess. And you?"

"I'm sick. Just realized it this morning. Sore throat and all that."

"Yeah. The sore throat sucks." Christina nodded. "It goes away in a few days, though. When the fever starts. Not that that's much better."

Someone close by started crying. Christina rolled her eyes. "Like crying ever helps anything."

Maybe not, but I was getting closer and closer to that same edge of fear.

The baby was still wailing, his cries mixed in with coughs that made me close my eyes. He was sick, too. How long would a baby last in this bus, without fresh air?

"Where are they taking us?" Mom asked.

"I think this bus goes to Levelry Center."

"Where is it?"

"No idea. But I figure if they want to arrive with at least a few people still alive, it can't be too much farther."

Her words chilled me despite the warmth coming from so many people packed so tightly. She had to be exaggerating. They couldn't let us all die.

I turned back to the boy in the corner. But if they allowed one person to die, one child, without anyone in charge doing a single thing about it, what would they care about the rest of us?

* * * *

By mom's watch, we'd been on the bus for four hours when we heard the first person's bowels give away in a gush.

"I'm sorry," the man said. "I couldn't hold it in anymore."

We were too far away from him to be affected, but I heard the sighs and groans of disgust at the other end of the bus. There, where the baby was.

Christina had somehow managed to doze off grasping the bar, her head drooping against her suspended arm.

Someone near me had an ereader that gave off pretty potent light, so I turned my phone off to save batteries. I'd forgotten to pack my charger, of course.

Mom and I, like pretty much everyone in the bus, had taken the masks off. It was too hot to wear them and besides, they did nothing to hold back the smell that was growing stronger as the hours passed.

Thirst, right now, was my battle. My mouth was so dry and hot I expected to see sparks with every breath I exhaled.

"How are you feeling?" Mom asked.

"I'm all right. Thirsty."

"Yeah, me, too." She checked her cell again and sighed. "I don't understand what's happening."

I took her free hand in mine and clenched it, not knowing what else to say. I was too thirsty to speak anyway.

Two hours later, the bus stopped moving.

"Maybe we're here already," someone said.

I leaned forward and nudged Christina, who'd been moaning in her sleep for a few minutes. Her head came up immediately, but her eyes were too shiny, even in the gloom. Her whole body radiated heat.

"Christina, we've stopped."

She nodded. "For water."

The word alone made the thirst, which I'd managed to corral in the back of my mind, spring to full attention.

The people at the back began to stir, and the cries and groans started again. I turned to the corner. The boy was completely still. I didn't know if he was still alive until his mom knelt down and whispered something in his ear. His only movement was a quick blink.

The door rumbled open, bringing a man silhouetted against the late afternoon sunlight, carrying, from the looks of it, a bucket. He said nothing, but started dipping plastic, disposable cups into it and passing them to everyone around him.

The people closest to the door lunged forward and started to drain their cups, taking each that was given to them and drinking those, too.

"Wait, they're supposed to pass those back here," I said. "Hey! Pass the cups down!"

A woman turned, holding two cups, and after a second of hesitation, handed them to the person behind her.

Finally a few cups made it to us. The water was luke-warm and tasted like pool water, but I finished it in only a few swallows. People were struggling to get to the front, but the ones closest to the door pushed right back.

The woman with the dying son had forced her way as far forward as she could and managed to get a cup. Would her son even be able to drink it?

I shook the plastic cup against my mouth to drain every last drop.

"Have mine," Mom said.

"No. You drink it."

"I'm fine. You're sick."

"Mom, I can't have you fainting on me. Just drink the water."

With a shake of her head, she did as I said.

My body cried for more water, yearning to grab another share, but the few cups that were making it to the back of the bus were slowly dwindling. After four or five more, they stopped.

"We didn't get any!" a voice cried.

But the man at the door was retreating, locking us in again.

Voices rose in protest as the darkness and the heat fell on us once more until the sound pulsed painfully against my ears.

"Your group is worse," Christina said, pointing to the crowd who'd come in with Mom and me. Shame, hot and slick, coated my insides even though I had nothing to do with those people. I didn't know a single one of them. "The group before passed the cups down."

"Where are they now?" Mom asked.

"They were dropped off at another center on the way to pick you up."

The baby in the back screamed. His mother tried to hush him, her voice thick with tears or sickness, or both.

"Will they bring us dinner?" I asked.

"They'll bring us something. I don't know if you'd call it dinner," Christina said. Her hair, blonde from what I could see in the periodic electronic light, was dampening.

Mom seemed to notice the same thing. "You're feverish."

"Yeah, it's been off and on for the past day."

Mom reached out her free hand and patted her arm. "We'll get to the center soon. I'm sure of it."

Christina sighed. "Yeah, then everything will be better."

I couldn't be completely sure since I didn't have a good view of her, but I could have sworn she rolled her eyes.

Chapter Seven

It was nine when the bus stopped again and the man returned, carrying two buckets instead of one.

The whole thing started again, except this time with slices of bread. The ones at the front got two, sometimes three servings, while the ones at the back cried out for their portions.

"Hey! Pass those down!" Christina screamed in a voice I hadn't imagined she had until then. It sliced through the bus, even drawing the man's attention from the door.

With a rifle he had propped to the side, he motioned for the front group to pass the food down. They did as they were told.

As I chewed the dry husk that was at least two days old, I saw the boy's young mother push her way forward again, a mask of fierce determination on her face. She snatched a slice of bread and stood still, waiting for the water to come down the line again.

I followed her with my eyes as she grabbed a cup and walked back to her son. I sipped my own water as she took a piece of bread and put it in her mouth, not chewing it but moistening it, then brought it back out and rolled it into a ball that her boy might be able to chew.

My breath hitched and the tears I'd been pushing back found their way out.

"Don't look at him anymore, Maya. It's pointless," Christina said.

The bus turned on again and lurched forward.

A large woman with huge patches of sweat on her shirt stretched her hand out to the woman with the dying son.

"He's beyond help. He'll die in a few hours. Give the food to someone who has a chance."

I thought the young woman was going to lunge and rip the other one to pieces. Her lips lifted like an animal's in a grimace of disgust.

It was amazing, how soon we turned on each other, how compassion seemed to weaken as necessity grew.

"Back off," I said. "Leave her alone."

Both women turned to me.

"Yeah, that's enough," a man said. "You already had yours."

The large woman, who, from the hoarse rattle in her chest every time she breathed was obviously ill, stepped back to her place.

Sighing, I turned away and hoped the boy would die quickly.

* * * *

Sleeping was impossible, not only because we were standing (I'd dozed off often enough waiting in line for something at school), but because of the noise. The baby's cries went unchecked for long minutes at a time, while coughs and sobs punctuated the darkness. Some people whispered to each other things I couldn't quite catch; I even thought I heard the cadence of prayer.

But it wasn't only external noise that kept me up. My head wouldn't be quiet either, throwing "what if" scenarios that left me breathless. What if we didn't get to the center soon? What if I got really ill in this bus? What if someone was sick enough to do what I'd seen Trevor do to his skin?

And then thoughts of home and of my friends invaded my mind. They were just as bad. Martin and Lisa hadn't meant to trap us in this bus, but their actions had caused it nonetheless. They'd been worried for themselves, I understood that, and I could sympathize, but the edge of betrayal had only been strengthened by the hours in this moving piece of hell.

I looked at Mom. Her eyes were closed, but I couldn't tell if she'd managed to doze off or not. She shouldn't be here. If she wasn't sick before, she would be soon.

My throat sent a stab of pain up into my head. The burning was getting worse, but at least I didn't have a fever yet. I knew, though, I would have one soon enough.

Turning away, I focused on the boarded up window a few feet in front of me, and willed the hours to pass.

They did, somehow, and morning came once again. To think yesterday at this same time I'd still been in my bed, not aware yet of the virus attacking my body.

"Did you sleep?" Christina asked in-between a yawn.

"Not really."

Mom shook her head as well. In her cell phone's light, she looked years older. "The smell is getting unbelievable," she said.

As soon as she said it, it really hit me, the foulness of the air in the bus. It wasn't just sweat and urine anymore, but other sharper, more cloying smells.

"They'll probably stop to wash the bus down soon," Christina said. "They just hose it with us still inside, so you have to press yourself against the walls as much as you can or get soaked."

So that was why the bus had been wet when we'd first got on. Not that it'd done too much against the smell.

But two hours passed, moving us into mid-morning, and the bus didn't stop, not for a hosing and not for breakfast.

"We must be getting close," Christina said.

An hour later, we realized she'd been right. The bus left the even, paved street it'd been following and started down another passage that rocked us every which way. Pot holes and rocks made us grab onto the bars tighter as the people in the middle lost their balance.

I heard the sound of water around us, on both sides of the bus, not the violence of the ocean, but lapping waves of what could have been a lake or a river. Where were we?

When we finally stopped moving and boots crunched on the gravel by the windows, we all seemed to hold our breaths. The door opened.

"We'll be moving you inside the center now," a woman said. Her accent was rough, full of sharp consonants.

Relief made my knees shake. Or maybe it was all those hours standing up.

"We'll take five people down at a time, in an orderly manner, you hear?"

We didn't need to hear. We could see her rifle well enough.

So she took the first few people down as the rest of us straightened up. Some of them were even smiling, as if getting to the center had erased the misery of the past day, or days. Even the baby had stopped crying

Five more people went down, then another group, on and on, until we neared the door.

"I can barely move," Mom whispered to me.

"I know. I'm so stiff." I tried to smile, but it shook on my lips.

The officer's voice rose above us. "If anyone has died, leave them there. We'll take care of it."

The coldness in the words felt like a slap.

I turned to see if anyone else had heard it the same way I had and saw the young woman bent over her son in the corner. There was no mistaking that stillness. She was holding his hand, and she seemed not to have heard anything. As I watched, someone tripped over her feet and she didn't even look up.

"Come on," Christina said, grabbing my arm. "It's our turn."

I had to put a hand up against the sun. It burned my eyes in a way I knew wasn't normal, even after spending a day in darkness.

"Move along," one of the officers said and gave me a slight shove.

That was when I had my first view of Levelry Center.

It'd obviously been a factory of some sort years ago, a huge, gray, concrete building with a thick, vicious looking fence all around it. It spoke of machinery and assembly lines. It didn't have the slightest air of a healing center.

The water I'd heard was a river that ran in front of it, all the way around the building from what I could see. On the river's other bank, the one we'd already passed, there was a huge chain-link fence blocking that way as well.

The only strip of connecting land was behind the bus. We were in the middle of a courtyard, right in front of the fence's gate, with two smaller buildings on opposite sides of the bus.

A scream made me jump.

"No! Let him go!"

I turned to look, but Mom took my face in her hands and kept it in place. "Don't look, Maya."

"Please!"

I recognized the young woman's voice.

I shook off Mom's hands and turned.

Two officers had the dead boy in their arms, one holding him under the armpits and the other by the legs. His mother was trying to pry their hands loose.

"Please don't burn him!"

I flinched. Was that what they were going to do? It was an efficient way of making sure the disease didn't spread, sure, but…

She scratched at their hands, making one of the men drop the boy's upper body to the ground with a stomach-twisting crunch.

In one swift move, giving no one the time to even imagine what was going to happen, the officer shot the mother in the forehead with his rifle.

Mom screamed next to me. Even Christina gasped. But I had no sound, no way of expressing the horror. A vast silence spread through my head.

The crowd around me shifted with fear, mouths opened and closed, but I couldn't pay attention to anything but that young woman's body, lying alone on the dirt.

"Maya." Mom's voice. "Maya, come on." She grabbed me and pulled me towards a bunch of tables I hadn't seen. My eyes were blurry and I had to blink a few times to clear them while we were ushered into two lines in front of the tables.

As we waited, Mom's hand was holding mine so tightly her nails were completely white.

"We'll be okay," she said, over and over.

How could we, after what we'd just seen?

"Names?" a guard with the same black uniform as the rest asked us as our turn came.

"Jenna and Maya Salaise." I was glad Mom answered, because I wasn't sure I could have said anything.

"Ages?"

"Forty-two and seventeen."

"Who is the infected one?"

Mom hesitated.

I jerked back to attention. "I am," I said.

The guard's eyes looked up at me. "To the right." He waved a hand in Mom's directions. "You, to the left."

Glancing to the side, I saw an officer ready to take Mom to the smaller building.

"No, wait. Where is she going?"

"Move," the officer said.

"Maya?" Mom's voice was getting higher.

"Why can't we be together?" I said, leaning forward so the guard had to look at me. "Where are you taking her?"

I knew the moment the man's eyes moved to the left that we were in trouble. The guard on that side took three steps and grabbed Mom by the arms.

"Hey!" I lunged forward but felt two metallic arms wrap around me and pull me backwards.

In seconds Mom had a gun pressed against the back of her head and I froze. I stopped trying to get loose; I stopped breathing.

"Okay," I said. "Okay. I'll do what you say. Just…please…" I couldn't bring myself to say the words.

And then the guard was pulling me away, forcing me to turn so I couldn't see Mom anymore. He pushed me past another door on the fence and towards the building on the right.

With each step, I kept listening. Waiting for the gunshot.

It didn't come.

Chapter Eight

They shoved me in a room bathed in white light. The artificial kind that felt cold, that carried with it the smell of iodine and ammonia.

There were many of us in the room. Most of us were teenagers, although some were younger. Only the guards seemed old enough to be considered adults, although, since the masks covered so much of their faces, this might not have been the truth.

"Take your clothes off and place them in those bins," a woman said, pointing to large plastic containers, "along with everything else you are carrying."

I spotted Christina a few feet away. She was clutching her pillowcase against her chest.

"Clothes off," the woman said, again. This time, her words were stained with a threat.

Slowly, the younger kids started removing their bags, their shirts and socks and shoes, everything they had on them, until they stood in their underwear.

"Underwear as well. We have all new things to give you."

Some of the older girls looked around, their faces creasing with shame as they saw the many teenage boys in the room.

But there was no choice, not with the guns and rifles in the room. We all knew it.

I bit my bottom lip and started peeling layers off until I stood, shivering in the air-conditioned room, with nothing whatsoever on me.

When every scrap of clothing was in the bins, we were pushed along towards one wall, where jets of tepid water blasted on us. A little girl a few feet away screamed in surprise.

After the bus, the shower wasn't unwelcome, and I was at least able to get a few mouthfuls of water before it stopped.

Shivering, we waited as a group of women, these without masks, handed out underwear of the most basic kind, tunics, and rough pants for us. Were these women also sick? Was that why they didn't use any protection?

The tunics did little against the chill, and nothing really fit, but at least we had something on. I rolled my pants' hems up to keep them from dragging through the soaked floor, and I glanced over at Christina, who was shaking with cold. She shouldn't have gotten wet like that, not with her fever.

And she wasn't the only one.

One of the older girls had wrapped her arms around a smaller girl, her sister from their similar features, trying to warm her with her own scant heat. It didn't seem to be working.

They shaved our heads next. Boys and girls alike, hair fell until we had nothing but a tight, short layer on our heads. I looked down at the clump of dark curls that had once belonged to me being already swept aside, already mixing with dozens of other clumps.

We were handed thin slippers that looked like they'd been used a few times already and were herded into another room which was completely empty.

"When your name is called, follow the guard," one of the unmasked women said, then turned around and closed the door behind her. A lock clicked into place.

Silence filled the room. The past few minutes replayed through my head: the coldness of the whole thing, the constant guns, the way no one looked at us, not even while shaving our heads.

I looked around. Everyone in the room with me seemed as confused as I felt, but no one said anything. We were all too scared, I guessed, and none of us had any answers to give.

Only one guy, about my age, met my eyes when I looked his way. He gave me the tiniest hint of a smile. I did my best to return it, though it probably didn't look much like a smile.

The door on the opposite side opened. "Carol Freemont," a voice called out.

A teenage girl walked forward. Her steps were sure but her eyes were pools of glittering fright.

I couldn't blame her.

After everything we'd seen, there was no way of knowing what was behind that door.

* * * *

Finally, they called my name.

None of the people before me had come back, which could mean a lot of things. But there was nothing I could do, so when I was called I just walked right through the door.

I followed a woman dressed in a tunic similar to mine but with one of the simple, black cloth masks on her face. She led me down two corridors and into a room the size of a school classroom. Instead of desks and chairs, though, there was a long aluminum counter lining one wall, with microscopes and half a dozen other machines I couldn't identify.

A guard, of course, stood in one corner, while a man dressed in a doctor's tunic sat on a stool in front of the counter.

"Maya Salaise?" he asked.

"Yes."

"Come here."

I looked to the woman who'd brought me into the room, but her gaze was locked on the tiled floor. From the corner of my eye, I saw the guard readjust his rifle. The message was clear.

Coming near the doctor, I caught the sharp scent of disinfectant, followed by the sweeter, if not pleasanter odor of blood.

"Stand on the balance."

I took my slippers off out of habit and stood on the cold metal.

"A hundred pounds."

I almost screamed as the woman called out my weight. She'd been so quiet I hadn't heard her move closer to me at all.

"That's no good," the doctor said.

I paused as I was stepping back into my slippers. The words made no sense to me. "What do you mean?"

He didn't even look up. "Mark her and bring the next one."

"Wait—"

"Take her."

The guard stepped forward and grabbed my arm, pulling me towards a small closet-like space I hadn't seen. Another man, in ragged pants and tunic, sat in front of what I recognized as a tattoo machine.

After everything I'd seen so far, in the bus, in the center, this shouldn't have been that frightening. Not after seeing someone shot in the head and having Mom threatened with a gun. But the idea of someone tagging me in some way, marking me like a piece of cattle, brought anger boiling up.

"No. You can't do this." I stopped walking. "This isn't legal. None of this is."

The guard twisted my arm until it felt like it was going to crunch in two. I cried out.

"Shoot her," the doctor said. "She's not needed."

My blood turned to ice water in my veins. They couldn't do that.

But I'd seen their violence already, I knew they could. And they would.

My legs started shaking, threatening to give up. I didn't want to die like this!

"No, I'm sorry," I said. "I'll cooperate. Please." I lifted my hands, palms out in a plea.

For a second, I thought he was still going to pull the trigger. My head was surprisingly blank, nothing, not a single memory passed through it. All I could focus on were the man's eyes above his mask.

He jerked his head towards the empty chair.

I breathed. "Thank you."

I did as I was told. I stretched my left arm out and allowed the man in the tunic to swab a piece of it with alcohol. I gritted my teeth as the needle dug into my skin and drew a letter, G, followed by a series of numbers: 537882. I didn't make a sound through any of it.

My arm throbbed as I was forced back to my feet.

"You're a softy, Len," the doctor said when he saw me walk back into the room. "Should have shot her."

Len chuckled, the sound distorting inside the metallic mask. Without a word, he led me out again and practically shoved me through two more hallways until I was in front of a huge metal door.

"In there," he said.

My throat and arm hurt too much and I was too scared to do anything but obey.

I pulled the door open and stepped inside, into what at some point must have been the factory's production area. The space was huge, or it would have been if it wasn't filled with people. Teenagers and kids were spread all around the room, some in clumps, others alone, but all of them were wearing a variation of the tunic and pants I had on and each had a tattoo on their left arm.

"Another one," said a girl close to the entrance. She made a mark on the wall behind her with a minuscule piece of chalk. There were so many marks on it already, it was impossible to begin to count them.

Not many paid attention to her, though. Not to me, either. A few curious eyes looked up for a beat, then went back to whatever they'd been doing.

"You might as well pick a spot. You can't stand there forever," she said, the bit of enthusiasm she'd been able to wrangle up already leaving her face.

I didn't know what to do. "What is this?"

"Your new home," she said with a chuckle.

There was nothing homey about it. Not at all. There weren't tables or chairs, or furniture of any sort, actually. A few people had blankets, the harsh, dark type you'd find in shelters, but not everyone did.

"I don't understand," I said.

But the girl had turned away again and started tapping the wall in front of her in a continuous rhythm.

My eyes traveled around the large room, looking for Christina or even that guy who'd smiled, just a little, so many rooms ago, but neither of them was here. I saw one face I thought looked familiar from the bus, but she immediately looked away when I caught her eye.

There really was no point in standing in the doorway like this, waiting for help that obviously wouldn't come, so I took a step, then another, until I was in front of the nearest group. By school clique standard, the group was pathetic, one teen boy and two girls, all of them in varying degrees of illness, but in this setting they seemed like an army.

I was thinking of which question of the many in my head to ask first, when the oldest looking girl, someone who was maybe eighteen, turned to me.

"What are you looking at?" She practically spat the words at me.

I blinked. "Nothing."

"Then go do it somewhere else, bitch."

Her companions laughed, the sound echoing through the room.

I froze. As a kid, I'd never been bullied at school. I'd never been the kind of girl with a collection of friends, either, but my swimming skills had kept me out of the whole bullying mess. Kids tended not to bother someone who might, at some point, help to beat another school's team.

So the wave of antagonism I felt coming from this group felt wholly new to me, filling my mouth with a bitter taste.

I did know enough, though, to walk away from them without saying anything else. Picking a corner that only had two other people, I headed across the room. As I walked, all eyes turned away from me, as if by not looking at me, they could all pretend I didn't exist.

I sat down and pulled my knees into my chest. The need to see Mom was overwhelming. I had to know if she was okay.

"Don't bother with them," a voice said.

I turned.

The girl was small, smaller than I was, even, with a face with features just a tad too close together to be pretty. But there was something in her eyes, a winter morning's blue, which gave her a look of sharp intelligence.

"I'm Lesley," she said.

"Maya."

"Nice name."

I sighed. "So I should stay away from them." I nodded to the group of three.

"Unless you want a nice bruise to go along with your tattoo, yeah."

"I figured as much."

There was a squeak of metal and another person, another teen girl, came into the room. She looked as confused and lost as I'd felt standing there. Without giving it too much thought, I lifted my hand and waved her over. The relief that flooded her face made her seem younger.

"Hi," she said when she reached us, the word just a puff of air.

"Hey, I'm Maya and this is Lesley."

"Jessica."

"Welcome, Jessica, to whatever this is," Lesley said, an edge of sarcasm in her voice.

"This thing hurts like a bitch," Jessica said, looking down at her arm. Her tattoo looked worse than mine, if that was possible.

"Yeah. It'll get less horrific in a couple of days."

I frowned. "How long have you been here?"

Lesley paused to think. "I think it's been two weeks, but I'm not a hundred percent sure."

Two weeks. In this place?

"You two look pretty good, though," Lesley said. She glanced at us, her light eyes as cold as the floor below us.

"I've been sick for only a day," I said.

"And I'm not sick. I haven't caught it yet, amazingly enough."

"Why are you here, then?" I asked.

"My dad. He got it from a coworker."

I nodded. "Are you sick, Lesley?"

"Oh, yeah. Past the fever already. My brother gave it to me."

"Oh. Is he…I mean…is he still…"

"Alive? I don't know. They separated us during the exam with the doctor. He went somewhere else and I was sent here." I saw a shadow darken her clear eyes.

"I'm sorry, I shouldn't have asked," I said.

Lesley shook her head. "We all have loved ones who are here with us, too, right? Everyone's going through the same thing."

"But why did they separate us?" Jessica asked.

"They always put the adults across the courtyard, in the other building."

The horror of that moment outside surrounded me again. "They put a gun to my mom's head," I said.

Lesley nodded as if it were the most normal thing. "They're getting worse. More aggressive. You're pretty lucky, though, because they have shot parents in front of their kids before. That girl over there…" She nodded towards a bundle of dirty clothes that I hadn't even realized held a person. "She saw her dad shot in the courtyard. She hasn't said much in about a week. I check on her every once in a while, but she refuses to speak."

I could imagine the overwhelming grief she was experiencing. I didn't think I'd bother talking either.

89

"So where did they take your brother?" Jessica asked.

"I don't know for sure."

I looked at my hands. "When they weighed me, the doctor said I wasn't good enough," I said. "As if he was looking for something in particular."

Jessica nodded. "Yeah, he said the same thing to me."

"He didn't want me because I wasn't very sick yet." Lesley shrugged and looked away. "Whatever. There's no point in obsessing about it. We're stuck here."

"For how long?"Jessica asked.

Lesley sighed and I had a guess as to what she was going to say before she said it. "We're not leaving this place except through the incinerator."

She could have said it with just a bit more tact, especially seeing Jessica's face fresh with hope, despite the surroundings, despite everything we'd been through so far.

In seconds, her face was bathed in tears.

"Look, I don't mean to make you cry, but it's the truth. You hear that?" She lifted a forefinger, pointing out a hum I hadn't really noticed until now. It was a white noise, continuous and vibrating. "They run the incinerator twelve hours a day. You can think whatever you want, but they have to do something with the bodies, and with the Tearings being as contagious as it is, there aren't many options."

"The Tearings?"

"It's what they're calling this virus or whatever it is. Have you seen what happens close to the disease's end?"

I nodded. So did Jessica.

"Then you know why it's called that."

"Has anyone died since you've been here?" I asked.

"Are you kidding? Ten kids, all different ages. But the thing is that most of them didn't die from the Tearings. It was dehydration or starvation, or even hypothermia. Others were attacked by the guards for minor things. I think only one actually got to the point of ripping skin off." She leaned back against the wall and looked at the two of us. "The truth is that we're screwed. Maybe the ones who got chosen are better off, but we're going to die in this place."

"So there's no medicine, no treatments of any sort?" I asked.

Lesley looked at me as if I were the slowest of the slow. "Of course not."

She shrugged, as if nothing applied to her. Had she already made peace with the circumstances?

Jessica sniffed and wiped her face of the last tears. Fear radiated off her like heat, and I was sure I was no better.

We had been lied to; the whole country had been lied to. But why? Just to keep the disease at bay?

Three more teens had come into the room as we'd been speaking, and they were still waiting there by the doorway, looking around with the same questions reflected in their eyes.

I was raising my hand to hail them towards us, when Lesley grabbed it. "No. No more."

"But they don't know anything, not even where they are."

"They'll figure it out soon enough. The guards don't like big groups, so they'll find some way of harming us so we'll split up. It's not worth it."

I watched the three of them move apart, walking to opposite sides of the room, as if they'd lost all ability to sympathize, to feel anything but the confusion in their heads.

* * * *

There were twenty new people in the room two hours later. Out of all the young people in the bus, only twenty of us had ended up here. The other ones…We had no idea where the other people were, but it couldn't be worse than here, could it?

Jessica and I, along with the other new arrivals, had missed the early meal, so we had to wait until night for what passed for dinner. Despite the floor and wall's hardness, I'd managed to doze for a few minutes when the voices started.

"Line up!"

"Come on, one line!"

I was fully awake at once, my heart beating so quickly I could feel it in my swollen, painful throat.

"It's just dinner," Lesley said. She was already on her feet and motioning for Jessica and me to get up. "We have to hurry."

My stomach twisted with the thought of food. I hadn't had a real meal in a day and a half. I hoped it was something warm, pasta, or soup, something that would make my throat feel less like raw hamburger meat.

Jessica and I followed Lesley to right outside the doorway, where two women in the same tunics and pants we wore were setting up a long table. They had no masks on, so I assumed they were already infected.

For the first time I got a good look at the rest of the teens who'd been in the room with us. Some of them looked healthy, if thin, while others could barely walk the few feet to line up. One girl, around ten or eleven, had to lean against the wall to make it out of the room. No one helped her. No one seemed to see her.

"Leave her alone," Lesley said, catching my gaze.

"But she needs help."

"If the guards see you, they'll beat you."

I frowned. "For helping someone else?"

"For doing anything that disturbs the bit of entertainment they have here. Betting on who dies sooner is something they really enjoy." Her voice had no expression.

I couldn't tear my eyes off the girl, but I also saw the guards that surrounded us and I didn't walk towards her.

The line formed quickly, without issues. Surprising, really.

I peeked ahead, trying to see what the men brought in the large baskets and canisters, but I couldn't make anything out.

"Take your food and don't say anything," Lesley said to both of us. "Just head straight back inside."

Everyone seemed to have gotten that same advice at some point, because they all hurried back through the doorway. Finally, our turn came.

One of the women handed me a plastic cup of water and moved me along to the other woman, who gave me a bowl of some kind of broth. It didn't smell particularly good, more like vegetables that were a few days past their sell-by-date, but it was warm, and that's all I cared about.

I did as Lesley told me, walking back as quickly as I could without spilling anything.

But I'd only managed to sit and get one sip of broth past my lips when someone spoke from above me.

"Give me the food."

Fear, like worms, burrowed through my body. It was the guy from the group Lesley had told me to stay away from.

I held on tighter to my bowl.

"Are you deaf? Give me the food."

Behind him, the two other members of the group, the two teen girls, walked up smiling.

"No, you have yours already."

"Oh, we've got a bad ass over here," he said.

I looked around and spotted Jessica and Lesley walking towards me.

"Get up," one of the girls, a redhead, said.

"Leave me alone or I'll call one of the guards."

The redhead laughed. "And you think they'll give a rat's ass?"

I looked around for help, but the few pairs of eyes I caught watching us immediately lowered back to their bowls. Even Lesley had frozen in place.

Jessica, though, walked up next to me as I slowly stood up. "Knock it off, okay? You guys have your food."

From behind him, the guy brought out a wooden stick. He held it up, as if showing it off, then brought it down against my knee, making it buckle with a crunch. I gasped and crashed into Jessica, spilling my bowl all over myself and the floor.

The stick came down again, hitting me on my left side. And one more time on Jessica, getting her arm. I waited for another hit, but it didn't come. When I looked up again, the three of them were smiling.

"Next time, you'll do as we say," the redhead said.

They left, chuckling.

"Are you okay?" I asked Jessica.

She nodded. "It's just my arm. You?"

"Yeah, fine."

But my knee was throbbing, pulsing with every heartbeat and completely overpowering whatever pain I might have felt from the hit to my side. I tried to put weight on it, but it hurt too much. I sat down again.

"I'm sorry about your food. You can have some of mine," Jessica said.

"No. You need it. I'll be fine until tomorrow." For now, the pain had swallowed the hunger I'd felt as well.

Lesley walked to us, carrying both Jessica's and her bowls.

"Bad luck," she said.

I grit my teeth. "Yeah, I guess. You could have said something, you know."

"There's nothing I could have said that would have made any difference. I've seen it before."

"Great. Good to know." It wasn't her fault, I knew this, but frustration and pain didn't make for very clear thinking on my part.

They sat down next to me to sip from their bowls.

"Are you sure you don't want any?" Jessica said.

"No. Thanks, though."

Lesley didn't offer.

Lifting my tunic's corner, I tested the spot where I'd been hit. I flinched as my fingertips brushed it. There was a bruise already forming.

But what worried me weren't the injuries themselves. Yes, they were painful, but they represented something much more dangerous. Aggression like this didn't just disappear from one day to the next, so what was to stop the group from doing the same thing tomorrow morning and night? And the day after that?

How long could I last, sick as I'd soon be, before I starved?

And there was no one who'd help, that had been made clear. Not a single person apart from Jessica had been willing to stand up to them.

As I leaned back, with a tunic soaked by cooling broth, I realized, fully for the first time, just how much trouble I was in.

* * * *

Neither Jessica nor I had blankets to sleep on.

An hour or so after dinner, the lights had suddenly turned off all at once, leaving us in a thick darkness unbroken by a single light.

At once, the unmistakable sounds of people arranging themselves to sleep surrounded us.

"You two can share my blanket if you want," Lesley said. She'd probably been feeling just a tad guilty about not helping me earlier.

But of course, three of us wouldn't fit under one blanket.

"You take it," Jessica said. "You didn't get to eat."

I wanted to object, but my tunic was still wet and I'd felt slight shivers running down my body. Great. Fever.

So I curled up as much as I could under the scratchy blanket and closed my eyes.

Without the cover of conversation to mask them, the sounds of sickness spread through the room. Wheezing and coughing, even moaning, rose up from the darkness.

I closed my eyes, but immediately opened them again when I saw the image of the young woman being shot in the head reflected inside my eyelids. I shivered.

And Mom. Where was she? Was someone sharing a blanket with her?

Was she even still alive?

My nails dug into my palms. I had to try to get some sleep. All of these questions, all of these worries would still be there tomorrow. I'd think about them then.

V.C. REPETTO

Chapter Nine

A shout yanked me up from sleep.

"Up! Now!"

The lights were on again and people were standing, not, apparently, as quickly as the guards would have liked.

"Up!" They screamed again, walking into the room and kicking out at whatever bundle of clothes was nearer.

"What is it?" I asked, sitting up.

"Roll call," Lesley said.

In a couple of minutes, we were all herded outside, back to the courtyard. The sun hadn't risen yet and the night still had a chill running through it. Or maybe that was just me.

There were already lines of people out. At the far end, close to the fence I assumed they'd taken Mom through, were the adults. They didn't look much different than we did, with shaved heads and tunics. I stood on the tips of my toes, biting back a groan at the pain in my knee, to see if I could catch sight of Mom, but there were so many of them! And like that, in the twilight hours, in uniform and slumped with illness, men and women looked too similar to tell apart.

We stood for minutes as guards congregated in front of us, most holding cups of coffee or tea hot enough for the steam to be visible from where we were. I would have given a lot for a cup.

"Why don't they just start?" Jessica said next to me.

"It's more fun if we have to wait standing up," Lesley said.

Finally, the guards, looking like slices of night in their uniforms, turned towards us. One, who had a large mole on his left cheek, brought out an electronic tablet of some kind.

"Karen Roberts," he shouted.

A young girl, one who should still have been tucked into the bed until it was time to get up to go to elementary school, stepped out of the crowd. "Here," she called.

"Bathroom duties," Mole Man said.

She lowered her head and walked to where another officer waited.

As I watched her walk, I noticed someone, a young man, standing at the very edge of the courtyard, almost completely engulfed in shadows. He watched the girl cross the square. He had a black uniform on, like the guards, but the mask over his nose and mouth was transparent. He stood impossibly still amid the courtyard's movement. A guard passed by him and gave him a small nod.

I frowned. Who was he?

Mole Man's voice calling another name drew my attention back to what was happening around me.

Roll call continued like that, person by person, minute by minute, the crowd slowly thinning as people were assigned to either bathroom duties, food preparation, outside labor, or main hall clean-up.

Jessica was assigned to main hall clean-up, as was the group that had taken my food the night before. I finally learned their names. Elize was the redhead, Kyle was the guy, and the other girl was Dawn.

While I waited for my name, I kept glancing at the adults across the yard, watching for Mom's name to be called out. Although I wouldn't be able to hear it, I might recognize her when she walked forward from where I stood.

"Maya Salaise."

Finally.

"Here." I lifted my hand as if this were just a regular day at school.

"Outside labor."

I turned to Lesley, who was still standing next to me, hoping she'd tell me what I was in for.

She met my eyes for an instant. "Don't take any of the food," she whispered.

Food?

But I had no time to ask anything else, since the guard was waiting for me to join the clump of people who'd already been assigned to work outside.

Most of them, I noticed, were guys. Oh, this was going to be unpleasant.

Roll call couldn't have lasted less than an hour and a half, so by the time the guards led us off to our assigned duties, my knee was a knot of pain that was putting up quite a fight. The walk out of the courtyard, into the bare, uneven ground was the stuff of nightmares, each rock I stepped on sending needles of pain up my leg.

We were led to a fenced in area five minutes away from the courtyard. The fence was a tall, barbed-wire structure with glass shards poking out from the top for good measure. But it was easy to see why these were necessary.

It was a plot of cultivated land. There were rows of leafy greens defying the winter months, some I could recognize as carrot tops, but others I had no idea what they might have been.

The guard, who, if I remembered his voice correctly, was Len, stopped us and pointed to twelve of us, me included. "Weed the crops, water them, and add fertilizer. The rest of you will be doing the compost heap."

A second guard unlocked the gate leading into the crops and we trailed him in. There was only one other girl with us, a thin, anemic-looking teen who I doubted could lift a fork, let alone a bag of manure.

By now the sun had spilled tepid light into the sky, not yet warming the air, but at least letting us see in front of us. Weeding in the dark would have been a disaster.

The two guards stationed themselves at different corners and watched as the obviously more experienced guys grabbed the few gardening gloves. They'd spread themselves around the plot of land already, into what looked like the usual formation. For how many days had they already done this?

"Work," Len said, making me jump.

Right. I had to work.

I started right where I stood. It was close to the fence, and therefore to one of the guards, so no one had claimed the spot. I figured it'd do as well as any other, armed watch or not.

It was no easy task kneeling. The first time I did it to yank a weed out of what looked like a cabbage, I had to close my eyes to not cry out. But the more I did it, and I did it a lot since we had to walk to a large garbage bin in the center to throw things away, the more my muscles and articulations warmed up. The shivering hadn't really stopped, but at least pain hadn't taken over my body yet.

Time got lost somewhere in that bit of crop. My head was bent so low, my eyes trained so hard on the plants in front of me, that I didn't notice the sun climbing the sky until a whistle blew.

"Line up," the guard closest to me said, and led us out, back towards the courtyard.

As we were leaving I realized there was a building, a separate one from the main one, facing the crops. How had I not noticed a building at the most thirty feet away?

Where there people in there as well?

I didn't have time to really look, though, before we started moving.

Making sure neither Len nor the other guard was watching me, I stepped closer to the other girl in the group. "What are we doing now?" I asked.

Her eyes flicked to me, then to the rest of the group. Her face had the look of cornered prey. "Lunch," she said, then sped up.

At the word, my stomach rumbled. I was surprisingly not thirsty, but the hunger gnawed on my stomach enough to edge on painful.

The long table had once more been set up in front of the main hall. The same people who'd been handing out the broth and water last night stood in place, this time with pre-sliced pieces of bread.

I looked around the crowd but couldn't see the large group that had been assigned to main hall clean-up. Elize, Kyle, and Dawn were either still working or they'd already grabbed their meal.

I squeezed myself into the line, my eyes glancing around me every few seconds. When it was my turn, I took the bread and the cup of what looked like tea and waited no more than the seconds it took to get out of the line before starting to eat. In large bites, I swallowed the dry bread, noticing and not caring, that some of the crust had the earthy taste of mold. The tea was even worse, with no sugar and so diluted it barely had taste, but it was warm.

I was drinking the last of it when the clean-up crew appeared. I spotted Elize first, with her fuzz of red hair, then the other two. Jessica came a bit later, searching for me among the crowd. I didn't wave. No point in drawing attention to myself, but I kept an eye on her to see where she would go when she got her food.

"Hey," Lesley said next to me, making me squeeze my plastic cup in surprise.

"Hi."

"Didn't mean to scare you."

I nodded.

"You got to eat?"

"Yeah. My group got here a little earlier than theirs."

Jessica had seen us and was walking towards us, careful to avoid Elize and her bunch.

"They're such assholes," she said when she got to us.

"Those three?" Lesley chewed a piece of her bread. "Yeah, they are. Nothing we can do about it."

A chill ran through me. Then another. Oh, not good. I tried, but couldn't keep from shivering.

"Give me your hand," Jessica said.

"What?"

She extended her hand in my direction. "Let me see something."

I placed my hand in hers.

"The fever is not too bad yet," she said, letting it go. "My dad had a worse one yesterday morning."

I thought of Trevor on that bus ride to the swim match. He'd been pretty loopy, his words slurring with fever, but he'd also had a cough. I didn't. Yet.

How much time did I have?

A thought made me pause. Time for what, exactly? More time to work in that plot of land, fighting for every bit of food? Like Lesley had said, I highly doubted any of us would be allowed to leave this place alive.

The incinerator's hum seemed to rise out of the background to confirm that thought.

"Outside labor, take your turn in the bathroom," one of the guards called out.

I'd had so little water in the past few days I'd not had the need to use the bathroom, but I knew I should take advantage of the opportunity now.

"See you guys later, I guess."

"If we don't get shot, sure," Lesley said.

I frowned. I really wasn't used to her humor, if that was what it could be called.

As soon as I stepped foot in the females' bathroom, I took the time to give a silent thank you to whoever or whatever had sent me to work outside and not in there.

To say the bathroom was filthy would have been kind.

There was dirt and other, less pleasant substances staining the floor and walls, and most of the cubicle doors had large chunks missing. There were about ten cubicles, all taken already, and six faucets without sinks. The water dripped right to the floor, making large puddles that mixed with whatever stained the floor. No paper towels, of course. Just the bare minimum.

I held my breath and stepped into a cubicle when one freed up, using it as quickly as I could. They flushed, at least.

The water coming out of the faucets was freezing against my skin and my slippers got soaked. I'd have to get used to walking with soggy shoes from now on.

As I stepped back out the door, passing by the female guard watching us, a large woman whose arms were a little too long for the rest of her body, I saw Dawn, followed by Elize. I ducked my head, but it was too late.

"What's the matter? Look at her," Elize said to Dawn. "She's a little scared of us, I think!"

I tried to get past them, but they blocked my way.

"Yeah, she's definitely scared."

Elize leaned forward and lifted a finger to my face. The tattoo on her left arm was right by my chin. I looked away. She pinched my cheek, pulling at my skin.

I gasped as Dawn twisted my arm behind my back.

Long-Arms was watching. Why didn't she do anything?

"You got away from us today. Not tonight, though. We'll see you then."

They both released me, shoving me to the side.

I put my hands on the wall to keep from falling. Elize's words dug into me, filling me with fear.

Around me, people kept walking, moving as if they hadn't seen what had happened. The guard's head was turned away, facing the bathroom. She had to have heard. Why hadn't she done anything?

I swallowed. My hands were shaking, so I clenched them together and started to walk back to the main hall.

I turned the corner and almost ran into someone. The person came to a stop a breath away from me.

Looking up, I saw it was the young man I'd seen that morning, the one with the strange, clear mask. His dark eyes were watching me, the slightest of frowns on his face. His uniform, a deep, rich blue instead of the usual black, seemed to pulse against his paleness.

"Watch your step," he said, moving back so I could pass.

It was my turn to frown. After days of being treated like vermin, his voice's soft tone, and his movements' politeness made no sense to me.

I risked another glance up at him and saw he was still watching my face. His eyebrows lifted in question, yanking me back into the present moment. With a quick nod, I hurried forward, passing him by.

It might have been my imagination, or even the fever, but I could have sworn I felt the weight of his gaze resting on me until I rejoined my group.

* * * *

The sun disappeared and the work day was over.

My shivering had stopped for part of the afternoon, but was now back. I wasn't really sure, though, if it was just the illness or knowing that Elize and her minions were waiting for me. I was even considering not getting in line for food, but I knew it wouldn't matter. They'd find some other way of harassing me.

We were back to murky broth and water. I took my bowl and cup and walked into the main hall.

Jessica and Lesley were already inside and I made the effort to smile.

I didn't get the chance to even say hi before Elize and Kyle stepped in front of me.

"Hand it over, little girl."

Kyle had the stick in his hand already. My heart was pounding and my hands had begun to shake again.

"The bowl. Now," Kyle said.

I handed it over. A voice inside my head shrieked for me to do something, to put up some kind of struggle, but I couldn't. Fear had taken my ability to do anything but obey.

They smiled and lifted their eyebrows.

"Good girl," Elize said and pinched my cheek again.

My face burned with shame when I sat down next to Jessica and Lesley. My knee sent a twinge of pain up my leg. When had I become such a coward? Or maybe I'd always been one and hadn't known it until now.

"Have some of mine," Jessica said, passing me her bowl.

"I'll get you sick."

She shook her head. "I woke up with a sore throat this morning. I've already got the Tearings."

I still hesitated. She needed her food as much as I did. But at the end, hunger won, and I took a few sips of the warm broth.

Lesley drank hers down in a few gulps without offering to share. I forced myself not to resent her for it. She was doing what she thought best.

A shiver racked my body. "Jesus, this is annoying," I said.

"Yeah, it is," Lesley said. She must be going through the same thing, the same chills and waves of fever, but she never showed it. She was strong. Definitely stronger than I was.

I drank my cup of water and curled up on the floor, leaving the blanket for Jessica to sleep on tonight. It was only fair to take turns.

Closing my eyes, I allowed the fever to take me down into sleep.

* * * *

We were up ahead of the sun again for roll call.

The guards took the same amount of time as yesterday, talking about who knew what, while the rest of us tried to stay on our feet. While they dawdled, I looked for the young man with the transparent mask, but he wasn't there. It was good to know at least one person could miss roll call.

Again, I couldn't pick Mom out from across the courtyard, but there was a tepid kind of comfort in knowing she was there, probably looking for me as well.

We were nearing the end of roll call when a scream cut Mole Man's voice in two, mid-name.

We all turned towards the sound, which had come from the far right of the courtyard. There was a shift in the crowd as someone, a young man, stepped out of it. He was grabbing his tunic's sleeves, tearing at them to get to his skin underneath.

"Damn," Lesley said next to me.

The guards were watching the whole thing with eyes drooping with sleep, as if they'd seen this a thousand times before. They probably had, but it didn't excuse their lack of action.

"Why don't they do anything?" I asked.

The still screaming young man dug his nails into his left forearm, somehow managing to puncture his skin and tear out a strip, a ribbon of bleeding flesh.

No one did anything. No one stepped forward to help him, or hold his hands so he couldn't rip himself apart anymore. He continued to pull at his skin, his screams growing louder and sharper until they seemed to dig into me like pieces of glass.

How was he still conscious?

I suddenly couldn't look anymore or I'd lose whatever bit of food I had in my stomach. I was as bad as the rest of them, I realized, turning my eyes away.

Finally, Mole Man ordered someone to shoot him. It was done quickly, with as little ceremony as possible. It reminded me of the videos I'd seen on how they killed cattle for food, the ones that had convinced me to swear off meat.

Mole Man cleared his throat, cracking the silence and stillness that had filled the courtyard after the young man's body had been taken away.

"Jack Whitney," he called out, continuing roll call as if nothing had happened. "Outside labor." On and on, until everyone had been called.

But I barely heard any of it. I just couldn't take my eyes off the bloodstain on the stones. It glittered there, a scream made visible.

* * * *

I wiped my damp forehead with an equally damp hand. Despite the chills, the sun bore down on the crops strongly enough to have made me and the rest of the workers sweat more than the previous day.

I'd been afraid I might be assigned to other duties today, but it appeared that unless there was an issue with a particular worker, everyone stayed in pretty much the same kind of work. Only when there were new arrivals, I'd heard, would lots of people get moved around. That was the only time we got a day off as well. It felt wrong to wish for more ill people just to rest, but I couldn't help it. I'd only been working for a day and a half and I was exhausted.

My eyes trailed across the crops, to the pile of carrots we'd been pulling for tonight's broth. The one I'd most likely not get to taste unless Jessica felt generous again.

I looked up at the building nearby to distract myself from a shiver.

What was in there? It wasn't crop storage, because I'd seen where the vegetables went. Into a basement dug into the earth that had the largest padlock I'd ever seen.

As I looked up into one of the windows, I thought I caught movement from inside. Damn, maybe it was one of the guards who'd seen me not working. I bent my back again and dug my hands into the dirt.

The sensation of being watched continued until we were herded off to lunch.

* * * *

I got no food that night, as I'd expected. The next day passed like an almost exact copy of the previous one, minus the screaming person ripping skin off.

I noticed people had begun to cough more throughout the night, growing more listless during the day as illness slowly overtook them, inch by inch.

Jessica kept sharing her broth with me, despite my protests. Okay, pretty weak protests.

We fell into a horrid routine that was only varied by the increasing symptoms we experienced.

I started feeling hot waves which a minute later turned into arctic currents, leaving me shivering and sweating at the same time. If this was really a flu of some sort, it was on major steroids.

The only thing that made me feel remotely better was a quick wash under one of the bathroom faucets. It was the only mode of hygiene we had, and I took full advantage of it every time I could. There was no soap or hand-wash, nothing but the cold water, but it was better than having greasy skin and hair. We might be treated like vermin, but I refused to look like it.

I was coming back from one of those quick "showers", shaking my head a bit to dry it, when I saw the little girl, the one Lesley had pointed out to me when I'd arrived. She was standing very still a few feet from the bathroom door.

By now, everyone knew everyone else in the main hall, by face if not by name, but I almost didn't place her. I'd only seen her swaddled in her blanket, or way in the back of the lines during roll call.

She was bent over, watching the floor. She heard me and lifted her head. Her eyes, slanted and dark, looked around, as if she expected other people to jump out from behind me.

"Hey," I said.

She looked away.

I didn't know if I should move closer or not. I had to get past her to make it back to the main hall, but I didn't want to scare her…though it seemed a little late to be worrying about that.

"Did you lose something?" Dumb question. None of us had anything but the clothes on our backs. "I can help if you want."

She looked up at me again. Her thin body suddenly tensed as a cough worked its way out. I waited for it to pass, trying to come up with anything that might get her to say something, just one word, to me. It shouldn't have been that important, but somehow it was. In other circumstances, this girl would probably have been chattering about anything and everything. I thought back to when I was her age, eight or nine. I wouldn't have been able to keep quiet on penalty of death.

"My mom (*was she alive?*) always says that if you lose something you have to immediately stop looking for it. Otherwise, it thinks it's a game and hides even more."

She watched me without blinking. "I didn't lose anything."

So much for that. "Oh." I smiled, though. She'd said something. "What are you doing, then?"

She turned away again, but stretched her left hand out, pointing at the floor. The tattoo on her skin pulsed against her yellowed ivory skin.

I walked slowly to where she was pointing and looked down. There, scurrying across the floor, was a line of ants.

"They look really busy," I said.

She nodded. "They're carrying food back to their home."

"Cool," I said.

Her eyes met mine again. "Do you like animals?"

"I love them."

"I have a dog who likes to watch the ants, too. He barks at them."

Her voice, so full of longing for her pet, started a simmering anger in my body. She should have been with her pet and with her parents, not here. No matter how sick or contagious she was.

My hands clenched into fists. "What's your dog's name?"

"Toby."

"That's a perfect name for a dog."

She swallowed. "I don't know if anyone is watching him."

I thought of Lisa's father forbidding her to care for her neighbor's dog. "Oh, they've sent people to care for our pets."

"Really?" Her voice held a thin thread of hope.

"Yeah. My dad knows all about it. He works for the people who do that." God, the amount of lies in that sentence.

But it was worth it to see the smile spreading across her face. Relief lit her eyes. "Do you think Toby's okay, then?"

"Positive."

"Good."

The incinerator's hum filled the hallway's silence. I hoped no one had told her what that sound was. There was no point in knowing something like that.

Let her think of Toby, who was probably dead, and not of that noise, which would eventually swallow us all.

* * * *

On the sixth day I woke at Livelry, things took a more drastic turn.

I was standing in line for the mid-day meal when the woman who was serving us, the same one as always, leaned forward just a bit and spoke to me.

"They get extra rations for what they're doing," she whispered, barely moving her lips.

I frowned. "Who?"

"Those three kids."

My eyes widened. "Why?"

"The guards like to have their fun with certain sick people. They've been betting on how long you'll last."

She handed me the bread and looked away, turning to the next person. I walked out of the line, clutching my bread. The woman's words were loud in my head.

They'd made a bet to see how long I'd last. They were causing me this kind of misery, adding it to the normal amount I'd already be feeling just from being in Levelry. It wasn't fair.

I'd taken two bites of my bread when something hit my knees from behind, making them buckle and sending me to the floor.

Wincing, I lifted my eyes and saw Dawn looking down at me. They were usually the last group to come out for this meal, though. That was why I'd been able to eat in peace for the last few days.

"You know, we're getting tired of watching you eat off your friends."

Kyle came around, stick in hand and knelt to pick up the slice of bread I'd dropped. It was soaked in the spilled tea, already sagging. He watched me as he crumbled it up to nothing.

"This will teach you a lesson, I think. Besides, you're sick already, right? Might as well make it quick." Elize winked at me and twirled her fingers. "Oh, and I'd consider not mooching off your friends. Who knows what could happen to them."

The three of them left me there, on the floor, my pants soaked with tea, my stomach an endless, hollow space.

The rest of the main hall clean-up group came out shortly after. This meant Elize, Kyle, and Dawn had snuck out early just to torment me. Or what was more likely, they'd been allowed out early. Someone probably had a lot of money staked on my quick death. Too bad for me.

Jessica saw me as soon as she got near the line.

"Oh, God, what happened? Was it them again?"

I nodded. "They just tripped me."

"But your food…" Jessica's face twisted with anger and she jumped to her feet, ready to chase after Elize and her group.

"Hey!" A guard, Len, called out, walking towards us. "What's going on?"

"Nothing," I muttered.

"No, that's not true, there's a group that keeps harassing Maya. They take her food."

Len's face was immobile, or at least what I could see above the mask was, but I thought I saw the glint of a smile in his eyes.

"Really?" he said.

"Yes."

"You want to know what I think? I think you two prepared this tale to trick us into giving you a second portion of food."

"No, that's—"

"So unless you want to end up in a place much less pleasant than here, I'd be quiet and stop telling lies."

Jessica's mouth hung open. Even after everything we'd been through getting to this place, she still thought we had rights of some kind. She still thought we were worth something.

"It's fine," I said. Wiping my hands on my tunic, I got to my feet. "We'll be quiet."

"You'd better be." He turned and left.

"He didn't believe us," Jessica said. "But he was standing right there! He must have seen what happened."

"Let's just go in the main hall."

Lesley was waiting for us at our usual spot, already finished with her meal.

"Have my bread," Jessica said. "You can't live on a few sips of broth."

I shook my head. "Neither can you."

"We'll split it, then."

I looked around and caught Elize's eyes immediately. She smiled and wagged her eyebrows in a taunt.

"No. They've threatened to hurt whoever shares food with me."

Even Lesley frowned at that.

"But that's…you'll die."

"I think that's the point. They have a bet with the guards." I told them the few things the serving woman had said.

"There has to be someone we can tell who'll do something about it," Jessica said.

But Lesley shook her head. "If the guards have a little game going on, you're screwed. They're the only ones we have real access to here. If they aren't willing to help you, then no one else will."

From her voice, I could tell she'd already given up on me. Couldn't really blame her.

"I'll save some of the bread anyway, and maybe I can sneak it to you at night," Jessica said, her voice resisting any objections on my part.

I gave her a small smile and leaned back against the wall. It was a lovely gesture on Jessica's part, but I doubted a bit of bread would keep me alive much longer than a few days with the sickness rampaging through my system.

I felt the cold needle of hopelessness forcing its way deep into my heart.

* * * *

"Tell me about your lives," I said hours later, as Lesley and Jessica finished their broth dinners and I sat holding nothing but hunger in my hands. I'd not even bothered to get in the food line.

"What do you want to know?" Lesley asked.

"I don't know. Anything." I thought of the girl and her ants. "Do you have pets?"

"I have a fish," Jessica said. "One of those betta ones. He's all blue."

"Is he friendly?" I asked.

Jessica paused, her brow furrowing in thought. "I think so. I mean, he doesn't bite or anything."

Lesley snorted. "Fish don't bite humans."

"They do." Jessica leaned forward. "One of my friends had a little goldfish, the cutest thing. One day she put her finger in to try to pet it and the fish practically bit it off."

Lesley and I looked at each other, trying to hold back the laughter. It was impossible.

"It's true!" Jessica said.

But we were gone, deep into laugher. My body ached with it, but it felt good. Normal. In the midst of giggling, I caught looks from the other people in the room, most of them frowning at the unexpected noise.

"We have to watch out for those fish, now, too," Lesley said when we could finally breathe again.

Even Jessica was smiling now. "That's what my friend told me."

I cleared my throat, which was now a bit sore again. My stomach twisted with hunger, and the despair I'd been feeling closed in on me again. I needed to stay distracted. "So, what did your parents do before all this?"

"My mom was a teacher," Jessica said.

"What kind?"

"A science teacher, at a middle school."

"And your dad?"

"He sold cars. He was pretty good at it, too."

I turned to Lesley and raised an eyebrow.

"My mom and dad owned a small store."

"That's nice. What'd they sell?"

"Fabric. All kinds of it, for sewing. It wasn't as successful as they'd wanted, but it brought a nice income. I supplemented it with what I earned at church."

Now this was something I hadn't expected. "Church?"

"I played the organ on Sundays for service and for the choir rehearsals on Wednesday nights. I was better at the piano, but I managed on the organ, too."

"That's so cool," Jessica said. "So you can read music, then?"

"Yup." She looked down. "I've had lessons every week since I was six. With the same teacher."

How would it feel to be able to bring music to life like that, with your own hands?

"I miss it, actually."

I looked up at Lesley.

"It's the only thing, apart from my parents, that I really miss. This is the longest time I've gone without playing. I know it sounds really stupid. I should be missing, like, good food and stuff like that, but it's hard to put it aside after doing it for so long." She clasped her hands together.

She'd probably hate me forever, but I went with my instinct and took one of her hands in mine. Her skin was burning to the touch, like clasping a flame. She said nothing, but she also didn't pull away.

"You'll play music again," Jessica said. "You'll see."

But Lesley shook her head. "I don't think so."

I didn't know if it was just the fever talking or if she had really given up.

When the lights turned off a few minutes later, the three of us curled up together, Lesley shivering in the middle.

I was almost asleep when something rough pressed against my free hand.

It took me a second to realize what it was: the piece of bread Jessica had saved for me.

Chapter Ten

Three more people collapsed during roll call the following day. Two of them on our side of the courtyard, the other one an adult. A man, from his height. As with the other guy a few days before, the guards shot them only after letting them tear at their skin for a bit, for entertainment value I imagined, then dragged them who knew where.

Lesley was worse as well. The fever had receded a bit, but now she had a cough that sounded like someone was sawing a piece of wood. It was painful to hear and, I was sure, much more so to experience.

The hours passed slowly, with hunger the only thing I could count on. I made another attempt at getting food during lunch, but I shouldn't have bothered. Elize, Kyle, and Dawn were always around, aided by the guards who wanted me dead.

Work, sleep, drag myself up, and repeat.

After another day, I realized I couldn't last much more like I was. As I'd imagined, a piece of bread snuck under the mantle of darkness was not enough to keep me from starvation's jaws. Not when I was already sick. By the third day of not being able to take any of the meager meals offered, my hands started to shake. I kept dropping the vegetables I was forced to gather, and walking back and forth between the main hall and the crops was getting more and more exhausting.

I could get water from the bathroom, at least. I had to be grateful for that.

But the fever spiked up as my body weakened, giving everything a blurred look, as if I were watching the world through murky liquid. The hunger was an unending cramp in my stomach now that seemed to be spreading tendrils throughout my body. I couldn't focus on anything, thoughts of food tumbling through my head, pushing even my mom's face to the background.

"We have to do something," Jessica said as she watched me stumble in during our midday break. "You're too sick to keep going like this."

But there was nothing to do, not as long as Elize and her group hung around, not as long as the guards found my slow death a thrilling form of entertainment.

We were getting close to the end of work later that day, when my hands locked on a carrot and didn't let go. It was a sickly looking one, with dirt on it, but I trembled with need as I held it.

I blinked a few times to clear my eyes and looked around me. Len was turned slightly away, leaning against a pole, and most of the other workers were so focused on their tasks they weren't paying attention to anyone else.

Only one pair of eyes caught mine. A thin, young boy around twelve was watching me. He shook his head slightly.

I didn't know what he meant. Would he turn me in? Or was he just warning me? But by then my head was only concerned with the piece of food that would end the pain in my stomach.

In seconds, the carrot was in my mouth, the tart taste of dirt blending with the sweetness of the vegetable, coating my tongue. I barely chewed, just swallowed the hard pieces until there was no more. Then I grabbed another one.

Halfway throughout that one, someone yanked my arms back.

"What do you think you're doing?" Len hissed in my ear.

But I couldn't focus on his words. They slipped through my mind, making little sense. All I wanted was down there in the dirt.

"She's really sick," someone said. Was it the boy?

"She is not allowed to eat any of this food."

Something hit my side and I moaned but had no strength to do anything else. Whatever happened now…I'd welcome it.

But Len didn't shoot me; he didn't even knock me unconscious. Instead, he shoved me out of the crop area, dragging me when my legs, weakened to grass stalks by illness and hunger, collapsed under me, until we were crossing the courtyard.

I couldn't remember the rest of it, but somehow I ended up being pushed into a black mouth that opened up in a wall. My legs and arms smacked against the cold floor, my head following them with a crunch. My vision blurred again as a wave of cold air shook my body, making my teeth chatter. But I couldn't lift my head; I couldn't do anything but lay there hoping the shivering would stop.

I was still staring when the only source of light in front of me closed, leaving me in absolute darkness.

* * * *

I woke.

No, was I really awake?

I blinked but the blackness in front of me didn't clear. If anything, it pressed closer into me, an almost physical presence.

My head was throbbing, but my stomach had quieted down to a low murmur. Shifting carefully, I sat up. As I tried to stretch my legs out, I smacked them into the opposite wall. How small was this place?

I stretched out a hand and began feeling around me. The ceiling was a few inches above my head, so there would be no standing up (not that I was truly considering that a real option with the trembling I felt in my legs), and the walls were close enough to only allow me to sit up like I was, or lay down with my knees curled up into my chest. Nothing else.

I had to be in some kind of isolation room. I knew I should have been more worried since these kind of dark, confined spaces had often been used as torture, but I couldn't muster up any feeling at all. Not fear. Not despair.

Sitting like that, my head felt better, so I closed my eyes and tried to clear my mind. In seconds, I was gone.

* * * *

There was a sudden squeak of metal that jerked me awake.

At first, I had no idea what the noise could have been, but I soon caught a sliver of light that was slowly appearing in front of me. Someone was slipping a plate through a slit on the door. The light disappeared too soon.

It was food, I supposed, on that plate, but after all the days of starvation, of overwhelming hunger, I found I had no appetite at all. It'd been replaced by this roiling sensation in my head. The fever was good for something, at least.

Still, I forced myself to stretch an arm out and grab the plate. It took an incredible amount of effort to do that much.

There was a slice of bread and a small plastic cup of water. I drank the water first, since thirst had not abandoned me yet. It felt icy as it traveled down my scalding throat.

The bread was harder to swallow. My mouth was so dry that it stuck to my palate, scraping it, but I finally managed to eat it all. By then, I was exhausted.

At least being in isolation got me a meal and time to rest.

I felt a little more awake, so I did my best to stretch as much as I could. I shifted my left leg, trying to find a more comfortable position, and felt something pinch it. I leaned forward, feeling the floor with my hands. My fingers closed around an object with sharp edges all around which made me think of a piece of glass. Why was this here with me? I turned it over and over in my palm, its weight reassuring and cool to my burning skin.

The last person who'd been in here had probably lost it. Well, it was mine now.

I tucked it in my pant's waistband. If I ever got out of here, it'd come with me to see sunlight again. It deserved it, for keeping me company. At that thought, I smiled widely in the darkness. Somewhere in my head, I knew the fever was taking over my brain, but it just didn't feel that important.

Time passed, or seemed to pass, then it would stop and I'd be awake again staring at the void in front of me. At periodic intervals I couldn't figure out because I kept falling asleep, the slit would open and another plate would slide in. I drank the water and ate as much of the bread as I could, then pushed the plate right against the opening. Someone always picked it up, but I was never awake to see it.

I started having strange dreams that would trickle out into my waking moments. Mom was in most of them, but she didn't look like how I'd last seen her. Her hair was shaved to a thin covering, like mine, and she was wearing a tunic that was as stained as mine. She pressed a hand to my cheek, and it was cool and damp, like a wet cloth. It brought such relief.

"Don't go," I said as she started to dim, easing back into the darkness. "Please."

But she always would.

It didn't matter, though, because if she wasn't there, then Lisa was, laughing and telling me all about school. "I've been taking notes for you," she said. "So you can catch up when you come back."

I knew none of this was real, but I couldn't push it aside. I didn't really want to, anyway.

Not until Mom appeared wearing one of the guard's uniforms. She'd come as always, placing her cool hand on my cheek, her tunic brushing mine, but in seconds her face shifted, the bottom half growing a black, shining mask. Her eyes burned with hate I couldn't understand. They wanted nothing less than to kill me.

I screamed. For hours. Or maybe seconds. I kicked out, trying to get her away from me, pain flaring up my legs as I slammed them over and over against the walls. She disappeared.

Shivering, I curled up on the floor, feeling something wet beneath me. I didn't know what it was and I didn't care. Sleep. That was all I wanted. I lost track of when the slit opened, and I didn't bother to stretch my hand out for the plate anymore. Sleep was enough.

But Mom kept appearing, this version of her that making me moan as I lay curled up in a ball. Her voice sharpened, pulling me awake, but her words made no sense.

Her hand was no longer soothing. It was a slap, or a pinch, something that prodded at my hot, trembling skin.

Now I pleaded for her to leave. "Please," I said. "Please."

Sometimes she came with shining instruments that pierced my skin, slipping right into my veins and tearing at them. I felt my blood pouring out in gushes.

Fear consumed me.

I was lying like this after another attack when a deep voice came into the dark room. "Maya," it said.

It was familiar. Whose was it?

"Maya, sit up."

Suddenly, I recognized it. It was Derek's voice. What was he doing here?

"Derek?"

"Sit up, Maya. Stretch your hand out and grab the water." His voice was so soft and full of concern, like the last time I'd heard it.

"No, I'm tired."

"You can sleep right after, but you have to drink and eat. Do it."

I made the effort for him. I probably owed him that, at least, since I'd gotten sick and brought the woman he loved into this place. That thought brought Mom's image forward, making me moan with fear.

"Don't pay attention to her," Derek said. "Drink and eat."

I spilled some of the water as I brought it to my lips, but I managed to get a good amount in me. It was so cold.

I tore the bread into little pieces so I could swallow without choking. My stomach twisted and I thought I was going to bring the food and water right back up. Breathing slowly, I waited for the sensation to pass.

A cool set of lips pressed against my forehead. "Good, Maya. Good."

I smiled and slipped back into sleep.

* * * *

The next time I woke, there was light in the room. Well, no, that wasn't right, because I wasn't in the small room anymore, but back in the main hall.

"Hey."

I turned my head and saw Jessica sitting next to me. Opening my mouth, I tried to answer her, but nothing came out.

"Here, have some water."

I nodded. Jessica propped my upper body up and placed the plastic cup against my lips. As soon as the liquid trickled out, I realized how thirsty I was.

"Wait, don't drink it all at once or you'll make yourself sick."

She was right, but it took all my will not to reach out and gulp the rest of it. Slowly, I sipped, relishing every mouthful, until the cup was empty. I tried my voice again.

"Thanks." I sounded like two fingernail buffers rubbing together.

Jessica was staring at me, a small frown on her face. "We thought you were dead."

"So did I." I swallowed the soreness down.

"When the woman said you weren't eating or drinking anymore, we knew—"

"What woman?" Visions of my mother in the black uniform flashed in my head, sending chills down my back.

"The one who serves our meals," Jessica said. "I think her name is Meredith. The guards ordered her to take some food up to the person in the isolation room.

She didn't know it was you, at first, but when she didn't see you at all in the next few days, she asked us. All we knew from the other girl in your work group was that you hadn't been shot out in the crops. We had no idea where you were." Jessica frowned. "Meredith said you were eating and drinking up to a couple of days ago. When you stopped, she assumed you were dead."

"That's a pretty drastic assumption," I said.

"Not really. At least not here. She did as she was told and reported it to the guards. Then this afternoon, on her way to the adult's side of the courtyard, she passed by the isolation room, peeked inside, and saw that the last plate she'd left there was empty." Jessica cocked her head. "What happened to you in there? Why did you stop eating?"

"I had no strength left, I think. I don't know. The fever was really bad. I got awful nightmares."

Jessica shook her head. "I'm surprised you're still sane after spending so much time in complete darkness."

"Why? How long was I in there?"

"Almost a week."

I'd lost a week in that place? Anger coursed through me, boiling my insides.

"I guess a lot of guards lost the bet, then," I said.

"Yeah. Maybe now they'll leave you alone."

It was a nice thought, but I wasn't so sure about it. What would stop them from betting again?

Suddenly, I caught sight of Lesley walking towards us. She wasn't exactly smiling when she saw I was awake, but I caught the slightest trace of a smirk on her lips.

"Well," she said when she sat down next to us. "You're finally awake. You don't look as bad as I thought you would."

I did my best to smile. The truth was that the fever was still tugging at me. I felt better than I had in the isolation room, of course, but far, far from fine.

"You don't look too bad, either," I said.

Lesley smiled. "My fever's practically gone, but now I have to put up with the coughing. There's just so much fun you have to look forward to."

"And you?" I turned to Jessica.

"Still just my throat."

Jessica tensed as she looked to her left. I followed her gaze.

Elize, Kyle, and Dawn were walking towards us, faces already smiling at whatever they were planning on saying or doing to me.

The surprising thing was that it meant nothing to me. Seeing them like that, itching to harm me, made no impression on me. After what I'd seen and felt in the dark chamber, the horrors my head had conjured up, whatever they had to say would sound pathetic. Why had I ever been afraid of them?

"Look who's back," said Elize in her pinching, sing-song voice.

"Hi, Elize, how's everything?"

I had the satisfaction of seeing her blink with surprise.

"What do you three want?" Jessica asked.

"Oh, just to see this little miracle that came back from the dead." Kyle's voice was harsh but it didn't accomplish scaring me the way that it had before.

Maybe I was too sick to care anymore, but I didn't really think so. Something had changed in my head while I sat there in the dark, tortured by hallucinations. There was just so much more to be afraid of than three sick kids.

I gave them a wide smile and twirled my fingers at them the way Elize had done to me.

The three of them exchanged a quick look, scoffing and snorting. "We'll see you later, girl," Dawn said.

"Sure." My smile grew even wider.

When they were gone, Lesley and Jessica turned to me, their mouths hanging loose with surprise.

"What was that?" Lesley asked.

"I don't know," I said with a yawn. "But it felt good."

* * * *

I was turning over on my side to find a comfortable spot in which to sleep, when I felt something pressing against my skin.

Vaguely, as if in a haze, I remembered finding a piece of glass in the isolation room. I still had it. Smiling, I brought it out into the darkened main hall.

The lights had been flipped off about half an hour ago, but I'd been too uncomfortable to fall asleep. Now, feeling the contours of the glass, the edges so untamed, I had an idea. I knew how I'd keep Elize and her group away from me. And if they weren't willing to do the dirty work anymore, the guards would have to finally leave me be.

Compared to the dark room I'd been trapped in, where the blackness had been heavy and absolute, the main hall was practically glowing with light. It came from out in the hall and through the many cracks in the walls.

I sat up, carefully scooting out of Lesley's blanket.

My legs were still so stiff from the days of hardly being able to stretch them, that for an instant I thought they would refuse to hold me up. But after a fit of trembling, they remembered their job.

I easily spotted the three of them, sprawled next to a wall near the entrance, legs and arms twisted together. Walking quietly, I knelt down next to them.

I picked out Elize since it was obvious she was their leader. With hands less shaky than I'd imagined, I leaned forward and pressed the piece of glass right at her throat.

She jerked awake. The movement drew a thin line across her skin, slowly turning red. It looked like someone had sewn a red thread around her neck.

"I want you to listen carefully," I whispered. "I don't know what your deal is, but you will not bother me or my friends again. I've had enough of your bullshit, so unless you want to sleep with one eye open every night, I suggest you never," I pressed the glass a bit deeper, "*ever*, mess with me again. Do you understand?"

Even in the gloom, I could see the hatred in her eyes. If she could have torn my eyes out, she would have. But I saw something else as well, a spot of fear.

"Do you understand, Elize?"

"Yeah."

"This goes for your buddies as well. One of you bothers us, and I'll do more than scratch your neck."

I pulled my hand back and stood as quickly as I could.

Elize's eyes followed me until I sat down next to Lesley. I lifted the glass piece again, rotating it so she could hopefully see its silhouette from across the room.

I declared the nonsense over.

* * * *

As I'd expected, during roll call the next morning I was switched out of outside labor to main-hall cleanup.

It wasn't such a bad change, not now that I had nothing to fear from the trio, and at least it wasn't bathroom duties.

My head was still a mess and my body ached, but it wasn't anywhere near as bad as it'd been in the isolation room. I was wobbly, but I was me again.

"Can you help me sweep here? Are you feeling okay for that?" Jessica asked.

I nodded. "Let's do it."

The little girl, Sophia, whose name I'd gotten from paying really close attention during roll call, lifted her head and gave me a smile while I was sweeping. I waved. It surprised me how happy I was to see her again. I'd imagined one of us would have made it to the incinerator by now. I was glad to have been proven wrong.

Kyle and Dawn passed by us, their eyes hard as they met mine, but they said nothing.

"Wow, what was that?" Jessica asked.

"We have a new understanding," I said and left it at that.

Her eyes widened and a smile grew on her lips. "Awesome."

And so a new routine emerged. A better one that made days feel less impossible to get through. I had my meals, scant as they were. The piece of glass tucked in my waistband was a shimmering shield that I could feel guarding me even in sleep.

Things were a bit better, for now.

But always, in the background, the incinerator hummed on.

V.C. REPETTO

Chapter Eleven

A few days later, we'd been working for a couple of hours in the main hall when one of the guards pulled the door open and shoved someone inside. Even with a mask on, the disgust on the guard's face was unmistakable. For good measure, before leaving, he landed a solid kick on the collapsed person's side.

All of us paused in our tasks. The girl who slept by the door picked up her microscopic piece of chalk and walked to her collection of marks on the wall, ready to add another one.

"I wouldn't bother," Kyle said. "He looks dead."

In that at least, he was right.

The young man sprawled on the floor looked about as close to gone as was possible without actually being dead.

Everyone waited for the door to close again before getting back to their work. Not a single pair of eyes looked at the body in the middle of the room; some workers were even stepping over him to pick up plastic cups, never even giving him a single look.

I looked around, catching only Sophia's gaze. She was frowning.

"Isn't anyone going to help him?" I said after a few more seconds.

Silence.

I understood everyone was scared. I got it. No one wanted more problems with the guards, I knew that as well. Maybe the young man on the floor was really seconds from death and no good would come from bothering with him, but all I could think was that he was someone's son or brother. Mom could be just as defenseless right now, and I'd want someone, anyone, to show her that she wasn't alone.

"Hey!" I called.

"What's the matter?" Jessica asked from somewhere nearby.

"Is no one going to acknowledge there's a person in pain right there?" I pointed at the curled up body on the floor.

People looked and turned away.

Screw this.

I dropped my broom and crossed the room to the young man. He was whimpering, his skin twitching slightly. It didn't look like the symptoms of the Tearings, but there was definitely something wrong with him.

"Maya," Jessica said. "Maybe it's better if you leave him alone."

I shook my head. No one would want to die alone in the middle of the floor.

Carefully, I turned him over so he rested on his back.

I recognized him at once. He was the guy who'd given me a small smile that first day. Even though he was much thinner and he had a scar running down one cheek, there was no mistaking him.

"Okay," I said, although I doubted he could hear me. "I'm going to drag you to the side, all right?"

I hooked my hands under his arms and pulled. It wasn't nearly as difficult as I would have thought, not with how light his body was. I dragged him like that until we were right next to the spot Lesley, Jessica, and I always shared.

"Here, use the blanket."

I turned and saw Jessica holding it out to me. "Lesley's not going to be too happy about it, but we'll deal with that later," she said.

Nodding, I grabbed it and stretched it out so it could cover as much of his body as possible. His slippers, as stained as mine were, did not fit under the blanket.

"Do you think he has it, too?" Jessica asked.

"I don't know. Probably." I brought my hand up and touched his forehead. It was cool. "No fever, though."

"That's strange."

His skin seemed to ripple with spasms that started and ended without pause. "It looks like he's having seizures, or something," I said.

"We better get back to work," Jessica whispered after a few minutes of watching him. "We'll get in trouble."

"Yeah."

I picked up my broom and started sweeping again, but I couldn't get my mind off the boy in the corner. What had they done to him? He probably wouldn't survive whatever it was. I shouldn't waste my time or my energy on him. I realized all this, but I couldn't just leave him alone like that. I wouldn't turn away again.

I checked on him one more time before we had to stop for our meal. I clutched the glass piece through the fabric on my waistband and went right up to the line. As I'd done for the past few days, I turned, looked for Elize and her group, and gave them all a wave when I found them. It was a calm warning not to forget what I'd promised.

They tried to slice me into pieces with their stares, but had no such luck.

I snorted. Bullies were pathetic anywhere. If you fought back, they retreated, tails tucked between their legs.

When it was my turn in line, I looked up at the woman behind the table, Meredith, trying to catch her eye. I'd thanked her a few days ago for coming back to check on me in the isolation room and she'd just nodded. She seemed like someone who just wanted to pass unnoticed.

She nodded now and handed me my plate and cup. But I didn't move out of line yet, leaning forward instead so that she had to look at me. There was something I needed to know, and since she seemed to have more freedom around Levelry because of her assigned duties than the majority of us, she might know.

"There's a young man who's just been brought into the main hall. He's unconscious, but he doesn't seem to have the Tearings. Do you know what's wrong with him?"

Her eyes flicked up to me and immediately looked down again. She fiddled with the ladle she used to pour the tea. When she spoke, her voice was so soft and so quick I almost missed her words.

"He was in the testing wing. I don't know what they did to him."

"Testing wing?"

"You have to go," she said.

I turned and realized she was right. A guard was already looking in our direction, seconds away from marching over to see what the problem was.

I walked out of the line and headed inside the main hall again.

Testing?

So the ones they'd separated from us were being tested?

"What the hell is this?" I heard Lesley's voice as soon as I stepped into the room. Sighing, I hurried over, balancing my cup of weak tea and tooth-chipping bread in my hands.

"Maya, no," she said when I got to them. "We have enough crap to deal with without you deciding to take in strays."

Every time I thought I was used to Lesley's harshness, she said or did something else that left me wanting to bang my head, and occasionally hers, against a wall.

"He's not a stray and he needs help."

"Well, we can't give it to him."

I sat down and gave her and Jessica a look. They followed my example, their bodies pulling closer as I told them what the serving woman had said.

"Testing? For a cure?" Jessica asked.

"I guess."

"So that's where the other ones ended." Lesley nodded. "I'd imagined it was something like that. But I haven't seen anyone else just thrown back in here. I actually haven't seen any of the others."

"Me either," I said. "No one mentions them."

The young man's body jerked, shifting his head to the side, and he moaned.

"What the hell did they do to him?" Jessica asked.

"They're probably injecting anything into their bodies to try to land on the magic pill that will end this craziness," said Lesley. "Probably pumping them full of pure Clorox."

Jessica inhaled sharply. I turned to her just as the first tear was trailing down her face.

Leave it up to Lesley to say the worst thing at the worst time.

I grabbed her hand and held it, sending pointed looks directly at Lesley. Finally, she caught on.

"I'm sorry. I wasn't thinking about you and your dad. Or even my brother, really. I'm just horrible at all this...sadness." She coughed lightly.

Jessica shook her head. "You're right, though. My dad is probably going through the same thing, which is another reason why we have to help this boy. If this were my family, I'd want someone to take care of him."

She wiped her eyes.

Lesley sighed. "Okay, fine. We'll do what we can for as long as we can. But," she lifted a finger and pointed it to her bread slice, "I'm not sharing my food."

I nodded. "Fair enough."

Chapter Twelve

The young man wasn't conscious yet when we all scrambled to our feet the next morning to head to roll call. I shook him with diminishing degrees of gentleness, but he didn't even stir. I had to check his pulse a few times to convince Lesley he was still alive.

"He won't be for long, though."

"Why?"

"If he misses roll call, it means he's too weak to work, so the guards will shoot him. I saw it happen with one boy who refused to get up the second morning we were here. They just walked in here, dragged him out by his tunic and shot him in the courtyard. As an example."

Her words chilled me. There was no way I could wake him and have him stand with us outside. I couldn't even get him to swallow more than a few sips of water.

"Maybe he's not on the list yet," Jessica said.

Lesley shrugged. "I doubt we'd be that lucky." She started walking away. "Come on, or we'll be the ones who are shot."

I tucked the blanket tightly around the young man. He looked a little better today, I thought. The twitching wasn't as bad and he had a bit more color in his dry cheeks. All he needed was time, but it wasn't something that was in my power to give.

I followed everyone out into the courtyard.

More than ever before, roll call felt unending. Minutes stretched as I listened for a name I didn't know, for a gap in answering voices. For the guards to realize someone was still in the main hall.

Mole Man called the last name and I could breathe again. They hadn't added him yet, we still had time to—

The guard's voice cracked my peaceful thoughts. "Great. It seems the Test Team has sent us a little gift." He snorted. "Just what we needed, another person to supervise." He lifted his eyes from the paper in front of him. "Is he even here? Tom Wells?"

The silence was only punctuated by the guard on the adults' side of the fence, who was still calling out names. As always, my ears listened for mom's name.

"Go check inside," Mole Man said to another one.

I almost didn't do anything. Despite everything I'd said to Lesley and Jessica, the easiest thing would have been to remain quiet and lower my eyes to my feet as they dragged him out and put a rifle to his head. I'd done what I could, right? I couldn't help him anymore.

But in the instant it took for the second guard to cross towards the main hall entrance, I'd realized that, no, I hadn't done what I could. I'd done a bit, right up to where it got difficult, and now that I was really needed, I was doing my best to back away.

I thought of Mom, and the young, fierce woman on the bus with her dying son, even of Derek, who had given me what comfort he could the morning I'd called him when all of this started. I had to do my best. For them.

Before I could think twice about it, I stepped out of line. "Sir, Tom is sick, but he'll be better soon."

Mole Man didn't acknowledge me, just continued flipping pages full of names.

"Tomorrow he'll be able to come to roll call. He just needs a little bit of rest."

Finally he looked up, though his eyes had barely landed on me before he'd turned away again.

"I don't give a rat's ass what he needs. If he can't work, then he can't be here."

The words were out of my mouth the moment the idea sprung on me. "I'll do his work for him. I'll do mine and his until he can do his own."

The silence from the group behind me was extraordinary. Even the guard walking towards the main hall had stopped and was standing still.

Mole Man laughed. It echoed inside his metal mask, spreading like a bad smell across the courtyard.

"You're bargaining with me?"

"No, sir. Just making a suggestion, that's all."

He was going to say no. I knew it. He was going to kill Tom and then me, for daring to speak up. Which was why his next words surprised me.

"And if I take your suggestion, what? You get your boyfriend or whatever he is, but what do I get?"

He was really considering this.

"Well, he can't get his meals yet, so I'd be doing the work for two people on only one set of rations."

"I don't care about food provisions."

Of course he didn't. Now what? There was nothing I could offer.

I thought back on all the days I'd been here, everything the guards had put me through... I blinked as I realized I already knew the answer.

"And, of course, it would be entertaining to see me doing double shifts. Fun stuff. You can all bet on how long I'll last."

His dark eyes held mine for the first time since I'd spoken. They glinted like knives. He held me there, in silence and waiting for at least a minute.

143

"Not bad," he finally said. "It really might be fun to watch."

I swallowed.

"I do have one condition to add, though. To make it more interesting for all of us. If you are not able, for any reason, to complete both jobs, then we get to take your life along with the boy's. That should make it really thrilling, don't you think?"

I heard a few gasps from behind me, but I had no time to pay attention to that now. Was I really going to agree to this? My mouth opened and closed but nothing came out.

The two guards started chuckling at my silence, exchanging glances that sparkled with amusement.

It all boiled down to a very basic answer: if I said no, Tom would die. Right now. In seconds and without having seen anyone he cared about or who cared about him again. He would end up being just the number tattooed on his left arm. But I had the power to change that for now. I'd most likely end up dead anyway from the Tearings. If I forfeited my life, then at least I'd die knowing I did the right thing, the humane thing, for someone else.

I nodded to myself. "Okay. Deal."

There were more gasps this time and I thought I heard Jessica telling me to stop.

"What's your name?" Mole Man asked.

"Maya Salaise."

"Fine, Maya. You start today." He skimmed down the list. "You are already assigned to main hall clean-up. And Tom…yes, Tom was assigned to bathroom duties."

I bit the inside of my cheeks. Yes, of course he was.

I nodded again.

"Good. Now get to work."

His mask covered his lips, but I was sure he was grinning like a coyote.

"That was about the stupidest thing I've ever seen," Lesley said in the seconds before she had to head over to the bathroom. I'd be joining her later, but for now, I had to start in the main hall.

"It kind of was, wasn't it?" I said. "I don't regret it, though."

"You will when you see the bathroom's state each day. I'm sure they'll give you the worst tasks, too." She shook her head, looking at me as if I'd lost all good sense, and headed off to work.

Jessica was quiet, unusually so, as we walked into the main hall.

"Do you agree with her?" I asked.

"I don't want you to die."

"Well, good, because I don't want to, either."

She bit her lip. "You don't know him at all."

"I don't need to. I just…I figured, they're not going to help us, right, so if we don't help each other, then what's the point in any of it?"

She didn't say anything for a few seconds. We'd already picked our brooms up to start sweeping when she turned and threw her arms around me. The handle hit the back of my head.

"You're not going to die. I'll help you in any way I can."

"Then, maybe letting me breathe would be my first request."

She gasped and pulled away.

I smiled. "Here we go, then. This is going to be interesting."

* * * *

Interesting might have been the wrong word. Vile, horrific, and nightmarish were all better and more accurate choices.

When I finally made it into the bathroom, Long Arms pointed me straight to the stalls.

"Clean them all. I don't want a spot on them," she said.

Now, I'd been using the stalls since I'd gotten here weeks ago, and they'd never been absolutely clean. It was definitely the hardest, worst task they could have assigned me.

My muscles, still weak from fever and near-starvation, groaned as I bent to lift the large bucket with ammonia and water.

"I'll help," Lesley said, grabbing one of the rags.

The guard spoke up at once. "No. She has to do it alone or it doesn't count."

Of course. "Thanks anyway," I said. I was glad, though, that she wouldn't be allowed to help, because her cough was getting more severe, and the ammonia fumes already wafting up would only make it worse.

I started working. My mouth puckered in disgust as I scrubbed and wiped, soaked and rubbed, watching as the grime and other substances I forced myself not to think about peeled off the tiles and cheap ceramic.

By the time I got to the second stall, the ammonia had forged a burning path down my throat so that each breath threatened to send me coughing. My eyes watered from the fumes so much that I had to wipe them every few minutes so I could see.

But I was doing it. It was slow and painful, but it was getting done.

When everyone got called off at the end of the day, I continued, ignoring my aches and the occasional chills that told me the fever was back.

Lesley put a hand on my hunched shoulder as she was leaving.

"Give Tom a little water," I said.

"I will."

I continued.

Two other guards joined Long Arms, one of them Len, as if watching me clean was the most anticipated sports event of the season. Biting down on the words I would have liked to say to them, I worked.

Ten minutes before the lights went off for the night, I finished the last stall.

Standing up, I dropped the rag, one of many I'd gone through during the day, and walked out of the room. The guards said nothing.

I'd never been so happy to breathe the main hall's air. Though far from fresh, it didn't have the sharp spikes of ammonia that dug into my lungs.

I stumbled towards our corner and lay down right on the bare floor.

"This is ridiculous," Lesley said. "You'll kill yourself."

I sighed. "Has he opened his eyes at all?"

"No. We got a bit of water into him, though," Jessica said.

"Good." I closed my own eyes and must have fallen asleep.

* * * *

Lesley's coughing woke me long before the lights came back on. It was a continuous, wet sound now that carried a chilling whistling after it, as if each cough was tearing a little piece of her lungs with it.

She'd pause for a minute or two, then launch into another spasm that left her gasping for air. I watched her body contract, knowing there was nothing I could do to help her. It seemed so archaic, watching someone cough herself to death, but it was happening all around me.

The other teen girl who'd worked in the crops had been carried away earlier that day, Jessica had told me. She'd sat down among the radishes and hadn't been able to get back up. And it would get worse as the disease advanced in all of us. Pretty soon, the guards would have more corpses than people to deal with.

I lay there, staring at Lesley's back for a long time. Only as a bit of morning light started to ooze in through the cracks in the walls did I turn to look at Tom.

I almost leapt up when I saw his eyes were looking straight at me.

"Oh," I said.

He blinked at me, slowly, as if he had to muster strength to do even that limited movement.

I had never seen eyes that color before. They weren't blue exactly, but more like pieces of glass with the lightest drop of blue spread out on their surfaces. Just hint of bright color.

And then they closed again, taking all their light with them.

I blinked in the still room. Maybe I'd been right, and all he'd needed was time to rest.

The shout for roll call pierced into the room.

Lucky him.

The day started out the same, with main hall clean-up, picking up the remnants of the meals from the day before, sweeping, mopping…the usual. I wasn't looking forward to bathroom duties, since I had no idea what they'd assign me to do today, but at least it wouldn't be scrubbing toilets again.

Tom opened his eyes one more time while the three of us were sitting chewing our bread slices.

"Hi, Tom," I said, watching his peculiar eyes turn from me to Jessica and Lesley, and back to me. His lips twitched in a hint of a smile, but his eyes closed again and he was dragged back into whatever world he was swimming through.

"He opened his eyes earlier this morning, too," I said.

"Doesn't mean anything," Lesley said with a shrug.

"It could mean he'll get better."

"Yeah, there's no need to be so negative," Jessica said.

Lesley chuckled drily, the sound morphing into a cough in seconds. When she finally gasped in air, her eyes were glittering with fury. "Just look around you. Look at where you are. I have every right to be negative."

She lowered her head into her hands and said nothing else.

* * * *

My eyes were lying to me. They had to be.

The stalls were filthy again, even worse than I'd encountered them yesterday, if that was possible.

"But, how?" I whispered.

My eyes flicked to Long Arms, who had a smile on her face. "You did such a nice job yesterday that we had to see if you could do it again. I'd get started if I were you, because this looks like it'll take you a while."

I had the urge to throw the bucket filled with ammonia right at her face, but I managed to control myself. It wouldn't help Tom or me to do something like that. Instead, I bit my lips until I tasted blood, and carried the bucket into the first stall.

From the smell, I could tell someone had spread a mixture of mud and manure liberally over every available surface. The sweet, pungent smell wrapped around me, twisting my stomach.

This was as bad as any of the nightmares I'd had in the isolation room, but as much as I pinched myself, there would be no waking up.

Chapter Thirteen

My nose was bleeding from the ammonia by the time I finished. My hands were so dry, so swollen, anything that touched them made me groan.

"Maybe if we put water on them," Jessica said.

"No. They've been wet the entire day." I blew on them gently. Hopefully the swelling would be down in the morning, otherwise I had no idea what I'd do.

Jessica had saved half of her broth for me since I'd not been able to stop for dinner, and she was holding the bowl up to my lips. She tipped the liquid, now cold, into my mouth so that I didn't have to use my hands at all.

"Thanks," I said.

"Maya?" A voice spoke up softly from behind Jessica and Lesley.

The three of us shifted to see who was speaking. It was Sophia.

"Hi." I smiled, trying to hide my aching hands.

"Here." She held out her dull gray blanket. "You need it."

I blinked in surprise. "Sophia, that's really nice of you. But don't you need the blanket?"

She looked over at Tom, still unmoving next to us. "You're helping him. You need it more that I do." She pushed the blanket towards me and I had to take it.

She accepted no thanks, no kind words of any sort, just turned around and headed back to her usual spot.

"Interesting," Lesley said.

"And very sweet."

I clutched at the blanket despite my swollen hands. Warmth radiated from it, and for an instant I felt that it didn't come from the blanket itself but from what it represented.

* * * *

Despite the bone-numbing exhaustion, I couldn't get to sleep. For some reason, the guards had left the door open and bright yellow light stretched along the floor, forcing its way into my eyes.

The more I moved to keep it away from my face, the less comfortable I got. But it wasn't the light or the discomfort that was really keeping me awake.

My head wasn't behaving. Thoughts of Mom churned through it and I couldn't get them to stop. Now that I knew about the testing wing, the thought that she could be in there, suffering through whatever Tom had, didn't leave me alone. Maybe I could ask Meredith tomorrow. If she was one of the women in charge of the food for the entire center, she might know where she was. The best thing would be to ask Tom, but I had no idea if he'd ever really come back to full consciousness.

Thoughts of tomorrow and what might await me in the bathroom also hounded me. Would they have me clean those stalls again? I didn't think I could manage another bout of ammonia fumes. Not that I had much choice about it, really.

I sighed and shifted my legs to the side.

"Where am I?" a voice said from my right, making me twitch with surprise.

When I turned, Tom was staring at me again. Not too much light fell on him from the open door, but it was enough to be able to tell he was more conscious than he'd been since the guard shoved him into the main hall.

"Tom," I said. An unexpected smile touched my lips.

He moved his head slightly towards me. "You're the girl I smiled at. The one in the crops." His voice was rough, torn by whatever had knocked him out for three days.

I frowned. "You saw me outside?"

He nodded slowly. "I used to watch you from my cell."

I thought back to those days, to the feeling of being watched, and to the silhouette I'd thought I'd seen. "So you were in that building nearby?"

He swallowed and winced. "Yes. Me and the rest of the kids. But I was the only one with a window, and I could see you."

I frowned. "There were only kids? No adults?"

"No. I think there's a separate place for them."

So I would have to ask Meredith about Mom.

A sudden shiver shook Tom's body.

I pulled the blanket up to his chin. "What happened to you?"

He turned his eyes away from me, then. Silence, the kind that was painful, that was heavy with thoughts, filled his body. "I am surprised I'm finally awake. I'd been dreaming I'd died over and over. I am awake, right?"

"Yeah, you are. To tell you the truth, I didn't know if you'd make it, either. You were pretty out of it."

He actually chuckled. "I can imagine." He turned to me again, studying me. "You look thinner."

Now it was my turn to laugh. "You should look at yourself in the mirror, Tom. I could probably play a song on your rib bones."

"How long have I been 'out of it'?"

"Three days. We've given you water and a bit of tea, but that's about it."

"We?"

"Yeah. Me, Lesley," I pointed next to me, "and Jessica."

"Why?"

"Why what?"

"Why did you help me?"

The same question everyone asked me, the one I asked myself over and over. "I don't know why, I just did."

His eyes locked on mine. It was unnerving when he did that, as if he could see right through, right into my head.

The same smile he'd given me that first day appeared on his lips.

"I don't even know your name."

"It's Maya."

"Maya." He paused. "Well, Maya, I guess you're stuck with me for a little bit longer. Sorry about that."

I smiled again. "Sounds positively awful. Now try to get some sleep."

"Yes, ma'am."

As I looked away, I realized I'd actually laughed. This boy, wounded as badly, or worse than I was, had made me laugh.

* * * *

I wasn't laughing, though, when I saw him trying to get to his feet the next morning. He was awake already when the rest of us got up, his back propped up against the wall as he tried to slide up and get his legs to hold his meager weight.

"Are you crazy?" I said, jumping to my feet. I ignored my own protesting muscles and took his arm. "You can't get up yet."

"I'm not going to lie here the entire day."

He gripped the wall. Sweat beaded on his forehead and lines of pain bloomed all over his face.

"That's enough," I said. "You'll hurt yourself."

"So he's up, huh?" Lesley said, lifting a hand to her head and rolling her eyes at herself when she remembered she had no hair left to touch. "Looks fine enough to go to roll call."

I shot her a look.

"Yes, I can go to roll call. I'm fine."

"You can barely put weight on your legs, how do you expect to stand still for an hour and a half outside?" I started easing him down onto his blanket, feeling every twitch of his muscles, every tremble.

Jessica was standing next to me. "Maybe it'd be a good idea to get him out there. We can prop him up between us."

I looked up at her, warning her with my eyes not to mention the bargain I'd made.

I considered her offer. Just thinking about stepping into filthy bathroom stalls again made my skin twitch. If we could get Tom to roll call, then maybe they'd release me from double-duty. But if he collapsed halfway through? The guards would shoot him right there, and all the effort to keep him alive until now would have been for nothing.

"Let's just wait another day."

"I can do it," Tom said, though it wasn't as believable as he would have liked since his voice was thin with pain.

I shook my head. "If you can stand tomorrow without losing every bit of color you have, then fine, but you look like you're going to pass out in about three seconds."

One of the guards shouted again for the stragglers to get out into the courtyard.

Tom's eyes fluttered, but he forced them open. "Go. You'll all get in trouble. I'll stay put."

Nodding, I motioned for Jessica and Lesley to follow.

Roll call was longer than usual, since three teens collapsed after only a few minutes of standing there. They were killed and dragged out. It was beyond belief, but not even the rifle shots shocked me too much anymore.

What did worry me throughout the two hours we were out there was Lesley's continuous coughing. She tried to suppress it, her whole body tightening with the effort, but it only made it worse. In one of the more violent spasms, she almost fell.

I could feel time unwinding for her, a spool of thread quickly running out. Then it'd be me and Jessica, and everyone else in this diseased place.

There was nothing to be done about it, though, so I pushed the thoughts aside and went to work.

My eyes travelled to Tom as soon as I entered the main hall. He was turned on his side and was shivering again under the blanket. I'd been right. He wouldn't have been able to last the entire roll call nightmare.

"You two," the guard supervising us said, pointing to Jessica and me, "you'll be waxing the floors today."

"Waxing? But they're cement floors!" I said.

"These are the orders I received. Get to work."

I looked at Jessica. Obviously this was just a way of trying to tire me out, to beat me down.

"I've never waxed a floor before, you?" Jessica said.

"Nope."

"Well, at least we'll learn a new skill."

I had to laugh. It was either that or run head first into a wall. I figured the former would be less messy.

* * * *

I could barely move my arms from the effort by the time we stopped for our meal.

"I'm surprised they didn't advertise waxing floors as a form of high-powered exercise," I said. "The gyms would have been packed back home for this upper arms workout."

"Yeah, mine are throbbing. Are they swollen?" Jessica lifted her tunic's right sleeve.

"No. But I know how you feel."

We walked over to Tom. He was awake again, and trying to sit up, apparently not having learned his lesson from this morning's exertions.

"What's going on?" he asked.

"It's lunch time," Jessica said.

"I'll share some of mine with you." I tucked the blanket a bit closer to his body.

"Share? They won't give you one for me?"

"No. You have to stand in line yourself to be able to get your food. Supposedly, it's to keep us from taking advantage of the people serving our rations." Jessica shook her head. "But if someone wants double rations, they have other ways of getting them." She avoided my gaze, her eyes landing instead on Elize, Kyle, and Dawn, who were already eating their food. They looked up as if they'd felt us watching them. I nodded at them then turned away.

Tom was trying to stand up again.

"Can you help me get in line?" he asked me and Jessica. "I don't want you having to share your food with me. You both need it."

I sighed. He was right. We were both getting to our bodies' limits and the less we ate, the quicker we'd get there.

"All right."

Tom gave me a crooked smile. It was incredible how much it brightened his face. "That was pretty easy. I'd thought I would have to wrestle you down before you agreed."

I snorted. "You couldn't wrestle with a fly."

"Ouch. That wounds my manly pride." He put a hand to his chest as if staunching violent bleeding. "But I guess that went out the window a while ago." He said it lightly, but I could hear the bitter edge of truth lining his words.

I leaned down and took his right arm, while Jessica took his left.

"Put your weight on us," I said.

Tom nodded. Slowly, we pulled him up to a standing position. His legs were still shaky, but they seemed better than they had been this morning.

"I'm always missing out on the fun," Lesley said as she approached.

"Yeah, and missing out on the helping, too," Jessica said.

"Not my fault. Talk to the guard who let us out late."

Her voice was as sharp, squirming with sarcasm, as ever, but there was something, a shadow on her face I didn't like. Fear.

I lifted my eyebrows in a silent question, but she looked away.

The four of us made it to the line, which was thinning.

"How are you holding up?" I asked Tom.

"I'm great. It's kind of nice to be carried like this."

"Yeah, well, don't get too used to it."

As much as he joked, though, he was still wincing with each step. Maybe he had broken bones. If I had time before lights out, I'd check if he had any fractures.

"Hi," Lesley said to Meredith. "Four rations." She pointed to all of us.

The woman looked at Tom and paused, bread slice in hand. "You're the one who was in the children's testing wing, right?"

He flinched as if he'd been burned. "Yes."

Meredith looked around for the guards, but they weren't paying attention to anything but the ball they were bouncing back and forth between each other. Their boredom was palpable.

"My daughter is in there." The woman's voice was fast, full of fear. "Her name is Helen. She's thirteen, and has a little scar, right here." She pressed her finger to the middle of her chin. "They don't let any of the adults in, not even to bring food. How is she?"

"I…I don't know."

"You had to have seen her. She has blonde hair. Or had." She was speaking even faster now, as if the quicker she let him know what her daughter looked like, the quicker Tom could reassure her that her daughter was fine.

"There were a lot of people in there. I'm not sure."

But he was lying. I didn't know how I could tell, but I could. He knew what had happened to Helen, and he didn't want to tell her mother. There could only be one reason.

"I'm sorry," Tom said. "She's probably fine, though. Most of them were okay when I left."

Another lie. He was unconscious when he was thrown out, he couldn't have known anything about the other people still left in the testing wing.

The woman didn't catch the lies, though. She actually smiled at his words, relief making her face younger, the way I was sure she'd looked before this whole thing started. She nodded and turned to the next person in line.

"Wait," I said. "Do you know if there's a woman in the adult's testing wing? Her name is Jenna Salaise." I tried to think of any distinguishing marks Mom had but drew a blank. It seemed impossible, after having studied her face for seventeen years, but I couldn't find any words to describe her. "She…I look a bit like her."

Meredith looked up at me. "I—"

"What is going on?" a guard shouted a couple of feet to my left. I winced. "You're holding up the line, girl. Get your food and go."

I tried to catch Meredith's eyes, but she wouldn't look at me. What did that mean? Was it just fright at the guard's looming threat or had something happened to Mom?

"Come on," Tom said in my ear.

We took out plates and cups and moved back to the main hall.

We ate in silence. I had so many questions, so many doubts. I wanted to ask Tom about the testing wing, to try to get an idea of what went on in there, but he was leaning against the wall, eyes down in a manner that welcomed no words.

"Maya," Lesley said. I was surprised to see she hadn't been able to finish her bread. "Can I talk to you for a second?"

"Uh, sure. I guess." Tom was buried beneath his own thoughts, so I just motioned to Jessica to come with us.

The three of us moved across the room, close to the entrance.

"What's going on?" I asked.

Lesley started coughing. It took a few seconds before she was able to speak. "The bathroom. It's really bad today."

Her words dug, icy, into my skin. "How bad?"

"Worse than any other day so far. There are three guards there today, and they haven't allowed us to do much of anything. They're leaving it all for you."

They must have heard that Tom was better. They needed to break me, today, before he regained his full strength and was able to get to work and get me off the hook.

"What are you going to do?" Jessica asked.

"I don't know. Work harder than yesterday and hope Tom is better tomorrow."

"Oh, he'll have to be," Lesley said. "You can't do this another day."

I didn't say anything, but if the bathroom was as bad as Lesley suggested, then I wasn't sure I could even out-last today.

* * * *

It was worse than even Lesley's cold words had hinted.

There was dried, caked mud on the stalls, the tiles, the walls. Every surface was brown with filth that had been sitting there, untouched, for so many hours it was stiff.

The guards were laughing behind me. "The rest of you can go," Long Arms said. "This is all hers today. You have until lights out, girl."

Lesley squeezed my arm, which was already sore from the morning's pointless floor waxing.

I couldn't do this.

I didn't even know where to start. Real fear bubbled up for the first time since I'd come back from the isolation room. I wouldn't be able to finish, not even close. I'd be dragged out and shot.

My thoughts stopped right there. Okay, I'd be shot. Or I'd live and die from the Tearings. Either way, I didn't have many options.

I'd do my best. There was nothing more I could do.

Taking a deep breath, I nodded to myself and picked up the first rag.

Chapter Fourteen

The last rag fell from my cramped hands when the lights went out. That was it.

I'd not finished, of course. Half the bathroom was still covered in mud and manure, although the stalls were done.

Kneeling down on the floor, I pressed my forehead to one of the clean walls. I'd expected fear again, but all I felt was exhaustion.

A bright light turned on, the beam of a flashlight pointing directly at my profile.

"Get up," Len said.

I grabbed on to the walls and slid up, my bones groaning with each movement. Someone grabbed my arms and shoved me forward, out the door. I was pulled past the main hall, and I wished I could have said something to Lesley and Jessica and Tom. I wished I could have seen Mom again.

But there was no point in regrets like these. They'd just make my last few minutes more miserable. I could at least spare myself that much.

The guards led me down a number of corridors, too many for me to keep track of, until we crossed a doorway and a light night breeze brushed my face.

I closed my eyes for a second, grateful for the fresh air.

But the air wasn't really fresh. As I breathed in, I caught a rank smell, overly sweet, like rotting fruit, and with it, the dark scent of smoke.

I had a pretty good idea where I was now.

This was where they brought the bodies to burn in the incinerator. There was no rumbling though, since it ran only during the daylight hours, but the smell was impossible to confuse with anything else.

Three other guards appeared from a door in front of me. All of them had rifles. Had they already decided who'd shoot me? Had they flipped a coin for it or was there some kind of hierarchy for these things?

I tried to still my thoughts. There was no point in obsessing over anything. I would prefer to die with a clear head, not one full of panic. A bit naïve, maybe, and even passive, but it was hard to strategize with four rifles pointed at you. If I'd had time to mull over this, then I was sure the worrying would take over, but right now I was so tired and I felt so ill, all I wanted was to sleep.

But I should have known it wouldn't be that easy or that quick.

Len came to stand right in front of me, so close I could smell his alcohol-laden breath. "You lost."

I lifted my eyes to his. There was nothing to say.

In one move, he brought his hand up, slapping me with the back of his black glove. The sting was immediate, but I didn't have time to truly register it before someone kicked my legs out from under me. My knees banged against the concrete with a crunch. My hands had prevented my face from hitting the floor, but I'd landed with such force I could already feel blood pooling against my palms.

"Get up," Long Arms said.

I almost didn't. They were already going to kill me, what were they going to threaten me with to get me to do what they said?

"Get up or we'll drag your friends here."

Oh. Right. They could use that. I hadn't known they were aware of who I was, since I only recognized one of the guards' voices. But I guessed the news had spread.

There was no wall around me and I doubted they'd let me crawl to the edge of the courtyard and grab one, so I'd have to do it all on my own. The pain from my knees was moving from hot stabs to cold shivers, but slowly, biting my lip until it bled, I was standing again.

"You thought you could do what you wanted, huh? Don't you know you're just infected shit?" A rifle butt crashed against my right shoulder, and I cried out in pain. It radiated outward like an aura, engulfing me.

"People like you are killing our loved ones with your disease," another of the guards said. I couldn't keep track of them anymore. The four of them seemed to meld into one horrific entity.

One of them brought out a stick identical to the one Kyle had wielded and hit my back hard enough to fling me forward a few steps.

"And what is going on here?"

I felt the guards turn, their hands dropping to their sides as they took in whoever had come into the courtyard.

"Sir, punishing one of the diseased."

With a shaking hand, I wiped the sweat on my forehead. I was gasping and I had a sharp pull in my back every time I breathed.

The new person, the one they'd call "sir", started to walk towards where we stood.

The other guards fidgeted for an instant, then settled into their military stances. I felt a giggle rising. This was so ridiculous. Why didn't they just kill me already?

"Punishing her," the voice said again. "For what?"

"She promised she'd be able to do jobs meant for two prisoners and she failed."

Not the most accurate of retellings, but whatever.

The steps drew nearer to me. I refused to look up.

"Really?" His voice was high and resonant, though he seemed to be speaking in a comfortable, easy manner. It was a voice used to being in command.

The next time he spoke he was standing right in front of me.

"Why would she do that?"

"To save another diseased person's life, sir."

"Interesting."

A hand, gloved, came into my line of sight and touched my chin. Carefully, but with a force that had to be obeyed, he lifted my head up until I could see him.

He was the young man I'd seen that first day, the one with the clear mask. I blinked sweat from my eyes.

He was around his mid-twenties, no more than that. His face was as thin as mine, but unlike me and the rest of the people in the center, the thinness suited his features, enhancing them.

"And who was this diseased who earned that kind of sacrifice?"

"Sir, it—"

"I'd like to hear it from her."

His dark eyes locked on mine. They were as cold as his gloves under my chin. They trailed down my face, taking my features in, appearing to analyze my every cell. I shivered.

"Well?" he said.

"He is no one I knew. He just needed help."

"Risking your life seems like a strange thing to do for someone you don't know."

"Just as killing people you don't know seems strange to me." I just blurted the words out without thought. *Nice going, Maya*, I thought. *Now he'll get in line to put a bullet through your forehead, too.*

But nothing in his expression changed. His eyes were still flat, glittering surfaces and even his lips, visible through the unusual mask, remained in the same half-smile they'd been in since he lifted my chin.

"What is his name, then, this boy who's woken this urge to save him?"

I felt my cheeks redden at the way he said it.

"It's one of the test subjects," Long Arms said. "He's one of the only ones who survived the last round. Though the last time I saw him, he looked pretty close to death, sir."

The young man's dark eyes flicked away from me only a second, but in that moment, I saw a tail of anger whipping past them. The glass quality of his stare cracked and re-fused itself in the span of a breath.

"Fascinating," he said, and stepped back, away from me. "Carry on, then." He motioned to the guards with a hand.

Until that moment, I hadn't realized how much I'd been hoping he would call the whole thing off. Reprimand the guards for abuse of power or something like that, and personally deliver me back safe and sound to the main hall. A scene right out of a movie.

So when he stepped away to allow the four guards to surround me again, I almost screamed in frustration.

The female guard came forward and tied my hands together with a piece of rope. Not sure why she was bothering. Even if I decided to make a run for it, I wouldn't get out of the courtyard alive, not with four rifles, and whatever gun the young man probably had on him.

The previous indifference and resignation disappeared from my head. Seconds away from death, there was too much running through my system, through my mind, to grasp. I wanted to grab on to Mom's image, but it slid from me until I felt the beginnings of tears.

That stopped me.

I refused to cry before these people. I would not give them the satisfaction of seeing me breaking down.

The guards were aligning themselves. They seemed to be going for an actual firing squad formation. The young man was standing a few feet away from them, just watching me and them in that same sharp manner. But I turned away. The last thing I'd see would not be unfriendly eyes.

Sighing, I lifted my eyes to the bit of sky that came into the courtyard. It wasn't much, but there were a few stars out.

I blocked the sounds out from around me, the guards' voices, the clicks of the rifles, and focused on the dark immensity in front of my eyes. I took another breath and realized it'd be my last.

"That's enough," said the young man.

The five of us froze in place.

"Sir?" Len said.

"I think that's enough entertainment for one night, don't you?"

"But, sir—"

"Do as you're told." His voice had grown chillier, enough to make me shiver. That could also have been the adrenaline at nearly having been shot. Yeah, probably that.

At once, the rifles came down and the guards broke up the line.

I didn't know what to do. Did I thank him? Maybe I was supposed to, but I couldn't bring myself to say the words.

"What's your name?" he asked me.

I swallowed the dryness from my throat. "Maya Salaise."

He nodded. "Len, put Maya in one of the holding cells for the night, then in the morning take her back to wherever she's supposed to be."

With a slight lift of an eyebrow in my direction, the young man turned around and left the courtyard the same way he'd come.

If Len hadn't grabbed my arm then, digging his nails into my skin, I'd have fainted with relief.

* * * *

I slept the night through curled up on a dirt floor. Surprisingly, I had no nightmares, no dreams at all, and when another guard fetched me the next morning, I felt more rested than I had in days. The only good thing about a near-death experience, I supposed.

Roll call was a few minutes away and the lights were already on when I walked into the main hall. Eyes turned to me, round with surprise, as every bit of conversation died down.

Jessica's scream broke the silence. "Maya!"

She actually managed to run towards me and wrap her arms around me. She was warm to the touch, too warm, but I was so glad to see her that I pushed all of that aside to worry about later.

"I can't believe you're alive," she whispered in my ear. "When you didn't come back last night before lights out, I thought…"

"I know. I thought I was going to die, too. I'll tell you everything later."

Lesley was also smiling, hunched over as she helped Tom walk to me. He looked less happy.

"I'm glad you're back," Lesley said. "I can't take care of these two by myself." Despite her rough tone, I could hear the relief she felt.

"Maya, can we talk for a second?" Tom said.

I frowned. "Sure, we can talk while we walk to roll call." He looked better today, less weak, and he was able to walk without as much help.

"You two go ahead," I said. "We'll catch up."

Tom didn't move or speak until Lesley and Jessica were swallowed by the rest of the crowd.

"Lesley is worse. A lot worse. She coughed practically the entire night."

I'd expected this. We were all sick. There was no stopping this disease once you caught it, so we knew the reality, but it was still difficult to hear when it concerned a friend.

"I know. Do you have any idea how much time she has before…before she starts ripping her skin?"

"A day or two, I think." He paused and looked away from me. When he spoke next, his voice was no more than a murmur. "Maya, why did you do it?"

"What?"

"That girl Dawn told me what you did to keep the guards from shooting me."

Of course she had, because leaving things alone would be asking for too much from those three.

"Why did you risk your life?"

I sighed. "I couldn't stand to see anyone else get killed in front of me. It was the only thing I came up with to buy you some time to get better."

"And you almost died last night."

"Yeah, well, I didn't."

He was about to say something when the last warning to get to roll call echoed down the corridor.

Tom gave me a small smile. "I know it's probably asking too much, considering the whole almost-dying deal, but I think I might still need a tiny bit of help walking all the way to the courtyard."

Smiling, I walked to him and let him put his arm around me. His breath brushed against my neck sending a pleasant ripple through my skin.

We were almost the last people to make it out into the courtyard, which was crowded with more guards than usual. We paused at one edge.

"Something's going on," I said.

There were even some people dressed in officers' uniforms like the ones who'd picked Mom and me up from our house. The memory stole my breath. How long ago had that been? It felt like a millennia. I didn't think I'd ever forget Mom's face when she realized I was sick.

Mole Man's voice broke through my thoughts.

"Before we begin roll call, there's someone you all need to know. He will be making some changes here in the next few weeks."

Was I the only one who heard a thread of bitterness in the main guard's voice?

"In three weeks, Captain David Summers will bring a camera crew in here, to record the center's functions for future generations, which means this place must be at its best."

"If you'll permit me," said a familiar voice. The young man from last night stepped from a spot of shadow in the courtyard, coming to face the entire juvenile group.

His eyes, sharp in the dawning day, traveled across the crowd.

They landed on me, and although he gave no sign of recognition, he held them on me for a beat longer than was necessary.

"As Johnson said, I am Captain David Summers. I doubt any of you have heard of me, but I was the one who thought up these centers when the disease really took hold of the cities. Although," he turned to around at some of the guards, "this is not exactly what I pictured."

Tom's arm tightened around me but when I turned to check if he was all right, his eyes were fixed on the Captain.

"Things will change while I'm here. The lack of control I've seen so far is astounding, and I intend to do something about it." His gaze landed on me again, and I thought I saw an eyebrow lift in acknowledgement this time.

"If these changes are for better or worse is completely up to you. If you cooperate, then things will improve; if you don't, then…well, I'm sure you get the point."

There was that word again: cooperate. But as always, what he really meant was cooperate blindly. Cooperate without knowing why you were doing it.

Captain Summers gestured to the building behind us. "I will be examining everything in there, preparing it for the cameras, but I will also be listening for those of you who like to cause trouble. You must understand that in a situation like this, there is no room for that."

I frowned. It seemed strange to hear that when he'd kept me alive last night. I had defied the order of things, after all.

"That is all for now, but you will definitely see me around in the next few weeks." He turned around without even looking at the guards and left the courtyard altogether.

Tom turned to whisper in my ear. "I don't like this."

"Me, either."

* * * *

"Wow, this place really is a mess." Tom dropped an armful of plastic cups into one of the garbage bags.

He was steadier on his feet, though he still had to use the walls to bend down, and he still got bouts of dizziness that forced him to sit with his head between his knees.

"Wouldn't it be smarter for us to have a garbage bin instead of just dumping things willy-nilly?"

I paused scrubbing a stain of indeterminate nature. "Wait, did you just say 'willy-nilly'?"

Jessica laughed.

"Yeah. There's nothing wrong with that expression. My dad used to say it all the time." Tom's smile dimmed for a second. "He used to say lots of things like that." He cleared his throat and picked up another bunch of plastic cups.

We worked until dinnertime in companionable silence. Captain Summers had not stopped by today, which was a bit frustrating since we all just wanted to get it over with, but we worked carefully. If he was going to keep tabs on all of us, then we'd better put on a good show.

When Lesley came in from the bathroom for dinner she looked weaker than I'd ever seen her. There was no color whatsoever on her cheeks or lips and she swayed when she walked, threatening to bump into the people around her. Not even Trevor had looked this badly.

The three of us exchanged a look while she walked towards us. She probably had no more than hours.

That knowledge stayed with me as I ate, watching as Lesley sipped a bit of broth then set it down on the floor.

When the lights turned off and we'd all lain down, I welcomed the oblivion that would let me forget there would most likely be one less person tomorrow and that there was nothing I could do about it. All I could do was clasp Lesley's hand in mine after she'd fallen asleep.

* * * *

Pain flung me out of that peace soon enough that night, though. I bolted into a sitting position, trying to find where it was coming from.

It was my chest. It felt like I had a needle in my lungs, digging deeper with each breath. A cough rose up my chest, but I managed to swallow it back down. So I was here already. I'd hoped I'd have another day or two before this next stage in the Tearings started.

I rubbed my eyes, waiting for them to adjust to the darkness around me. In my movement, I'd shifted the blanket Tom and I were sharing.

I'd thought it'd be uncomfortable to lie down next to a boy my age, but we'd both been so tired and dispirited that we hadn't had time to feel awkward before we drifted off.

Now, though, in the dark, I looked at him and felt the queasiness that accompanied my interactions with the attractive members of the opposite sex. Silly, considering the majority of us, if not all of us, would be making our trip to the incinerator in a few weeks.

As I watched Tom sleep, I saw him start to tremble. His whole body shook with whatever his head was making him live through.

I waited another minute to see if the nightmare would pass, but it seemed to get worse. His hands clutched at the blanket, enough that he tore a corner of it in two.

"Tom," I whispered, placing a light hand on his arm. "Tom, wake up." I moved him a little and he jerked up, gasping. His eyes were wide as he looked around him, trying to remember where he was.

"You were having a nightmare."

He let out a shuddering breath.

"I'm sorry if I scared you."

He shook his head. "No, it's fine. I'm glad you woke me."

I waited as his breathing returned to normal. "How are you feeling?"

"Fine."

Okay, so he wasn't in the most talkative of moods. Fair enough. I lay back down, feeling the needle stabbing down into my chest again. Maybe if I turned to the side, it'd be better.

The pain did ease a bit like that.

Tom lay back down as well, facing me. "You look like you're in pain."

"The coughing started."

He watched me carefully for a moment. "Are you scared?"

Was I? I was angry, bitterness at what was being done to us growing inside me every day, but scared?

"I don't know. I mean, not like I used to be," I said. "I used to worry about so much. Just the regular stuff, you know, school work and grades, making the swim team each year, buying a good present for the pickiest mother ever. Things like that scared me. Isn't that ridiculous?"

"No, Maya. It's normal."

"Yeah, I guess." I swallowed. "Now it seems pathetic. It's the only good thing about all of this. It let me realize how stupid I was before. If I had another chance, I'd not worry about anything like that. But that's not going to happen." I glanced at him, and it was impossible not to notice his face tight with memories. "What happened to you, Tom?" I whispered.

He lowered his eyes. He was quiet for so long I thought he'd fallen asleep. Then, with a voice hollowed out by sadness, he started.

"I saw my dad go through the entire disease, you know. He was one of the first people who caught it, in a mall's food court. I was there with him when he started ripping his skin off. I tried to stop him, but it was impossible. He was so strong." I could see the memory playing through his mind. "Since it was the early stages of the whole panic, no one came to get us immediately, not even when Mom started having symptoms. It was actually my school that turned us in when I got sick. We got here on the same bus you did and after they separated me from my mom, they sent me to what they called the testing wing."

Tom bit his lip as if trying to stop the words from pouring out. He suddenly took my hand, squeezing it with a force I didn't know he had. His skin was warm, smooth despite everything. Did he know he was holding my hand, or did he just need to grab on to something, anything, that was real?

He took another shaky breath. "They kept us in cells that only had hospital beds to which we were usually tied. They filled us with chemicals of all sorts, checking temperatures every hour, taking blood from us every day, taking sample after sample of everything they could remove without killing us. Kids screamed at night as the poisons they were injecting us with on the chance it might be the cure finally overwhelmed their organs. Sleeping was almost impossible. Our bodies could barely hold on to the food they were giving us, so that many of us died of pure starvation. Isn't that ridiculous?"

Tom's hand had relaxed its grip as he spoke, but he hadn't let me go.

"Then a new batch of drugs came in, ready to be tested. The doctors, actual doctors, went down the line of cells, pumping us full of this untested drug. It burned, Maya. Like liquid fire. I don't understand why they gave it to all of us, unless they wanted to get rid of us and get new, sturdier test subjects. If that was the case, then they were very successful.

"This drug, without even a name, just a bunch of numbers, killed everyone but me."

I thought of Christina. She'd been one of those who'd been taken to be tested. She was dead, then.

Tom continued. "It caused fevers and convulsions, unending ones. All of them, all the kids and teenagers, drowned in their own vomit. I don't know why I didn't die. I fell unconscious, I guess, and the scientists and doctors were so sure I'd never wake up, they dumped me here, for other people to deal with." He shrugged. "I'm surprised they haven't come to get me again since I did survive the drug. You'd think I'd be prime testing material. I guess they've forgotten about me by now."

But they hadn't. The guards knew exactly who he was, and now thanks to me, so did Captain Summers.

Tom continued, his eyes cast down on our clasped hands. "But I was lucky. Not that I didn't die, I don't know if I could call that luck or not. No, I mean I had a window in my cell. And through that window I saw you. Every day. For as long as they'd let me, I'd stand there watching as you moved, carefully, so gentle with the plants, even with the weeds. At first I didn't recognize who you were. I saw mainly the back of your head. But one morning for some reason, you turned around and looked straight at me. That's when I saw you were the same girl from that first day. The only girl who could manage to smile in the middle of all that confusion and fear."

He lifted his eyes away from our hands, and back to my face. "Strange, huh? That I could draw strength from a person I'd never even spoken to before a few days ago. You kept me alive in that cell. Even before the bet with the guards."

I didn't know what to say, so I just squeezed his hand again. I thought of that day, when I'd felt someone watching me out in the crops.

We lay in silence for a moment, separated by our own thoughts.

"Were you sick when you got here?" Tom asked.

"Yes. I dragged my mom here with me. She's probably sick by now."

"I had symptoms, too, but now I'm not so sure if I had it, since it really hasn't advanced the way everyone else's illness has. Maybe I just had a regular cold. Wouldn't that be pathetic?" He chuckled. The sound was light, no bitterness staining it.

I smiled. It was incredible the ability he had of brushing sadness away from his voice, from his face. And not only his own sadness, but easing that of the people around him. I'd seen him do it in the past couple of days time and time again, and each time it was as if he'd performed a minor miracle. He'd done it that first day by smiling, pushing away my fears, if only for a second.

Lesley started coughing next to Jessica. My body tightened at the sound, knowing she was getting to the end. And me, I was getting there, too. The needling pain in my chest pushed away any lightness I'd been holding on to for the last few minutes.

As if he'd heard my thoughts, Tom shifted closer to me, pulling the blanket over both of us.

"Get some sleep. Everything will look a bit less awful in the morning."

I wanted to believe him.

I really did.

V.C. REPETTO

Chapter Fifteen

I was trying hard not to cough. It was stupid, since everyone around me was already sick, but it felt like if I allowed the coughing to take over, I was giving in to the illness. Like I said, stupid, but there it was.

"Let's move that box over here, so we have more space," Tom said to a boy, pointing to one of the many empty, soggy cardboard boxes scattered around the main hall.

In the few days since he'd been awake, he'd taken command of the clean up, fixing things to make the space a bit more livable. I smiled as I watched him cross the room.

He looked much sturdier than he had even just yesterday. The little bit of food that was our ration seemed to fuel him more than the rest of us.

A few times throughout the morning, I'd felt his eyes on me as I worked. I'd turn and he'd immediately shift his gaze, making me want to roll my eyes. It was just like any day in the teenage drama that was high school, except we were as far away from that normal life of classes and crushes as we could get.

I was thinking of this, wondering what I should do about it, when we heard the scream. The sound, its pitch and color, was all too familiar.

Jessica froze in place next to me.

"Lesley," I said.

Before I could think about it, I broke into a run.

"Maya, wait!" Tom shouted from behind me. But I was already out of the main hall, running past the guard by the doorway and careening down the corridor to the bathroom.

"Stop!" The guard yelled as he ran after me.

I ignored him. But Long Arms, standing in front of the bathroom door, did not.

"What do you think you're doing? Get back to work."

Another scream rang out from inside.

"I need to go inside."

"No. Go back to work."

"No! Let me in." I tried to push past her, but she blocked my way.

"Maya," Jessica called out. She, Tom, and a handful of other people from the main hall had followed me. "Come back."

The bathroom door opened and a deep, gurgling sound oozed out, the sickening sound of blood. A young woman about my age stepped out. "Someone's died in here. She bled all over the floor."

I lunged forward again, but Long Arms pushed me back with her rifle butt. "I won't say it again. Do as you're told."

Someone laughed behind me. "Seems like the bathroom crew is going to have some more cleaning to do."

I spun around at the words. Of course. Who else could say something that cruel but Elize? Anger loaned strength to my starved muscles and I ran to her, my hands clenched into fists and ready to tear her apart.

The other guard, the one who'd been chasing me, launched himself forward and grabbed my arms before I could touch Elize. He kicked my feet from under me and I stumbled, landing painfully on the cement floor. As I kicked and tried to buck him off me, he pushed my face into the floor.

I felt cold, hard steel on the back of my head, but I still wouldn't relax. Anger burned through me. Lesley was dead. She'd died with no one who cared about her near her, without anyone even making an effort to help her. Grief dug its talons into me, making me cry out.

Suddenly, I realized how quiet the corridor was. The guards had stopped screaming. The only sound was my harsh panting against the floor.

"Get her up."

I closed my eyes at the voice.

"But Captain—"

"Do it." His voice was low, but it practically zapped with power.

Hands grabbed me and yanked me up, so that I could see Captain Summers and a few guards standing behind him. His eyes were poised on me, unreadable, watching me with the same cold calculation as a falcon would watch its prey.

"Everyone else, back to your assigned places. Now."

The crowd started to move at once, all but Jessica and Tom, who were shifting their eyes between me and the Captain.

"Are the two of you deaf?" Captain Summers said, flicking his eyes in their direction.

I gave them a small nod and they retreated slowly down the corridor.

"Now will someone tell me what all this nonsense was about?"

Long Arms jumped in. "This diseased came running out of the main hall, demanding to be allowed into the bathroom. Apparently, she knows the girl who just died in here. She also tried to attack another diseased."

Captain Summers said nothing, but motioned for the guard to bring me towards him. "Remove the body."

"Wait, I want to see her," I said.

"Be quiet." He grabbed my arm with his gloved hand and pulled me away from the guard. "You four," he said to the guards behind him, "make sure everyone is where they are supposed to be and doing what they're supposed to be doing."

"Yes, sir."

No one said anything as Captain Summers started walking down the corridor, pulling me along in his strong grip. His fingers dug into my skin, even with the gloves.

I walked until the guards could no longer see us, then started pulling, trying to pry my arm from his hand.

"That's enough, Maya." He tightened his grip.

My hands fumbled with my pants' waistband until I found what I was looking for. The piece of glass from the isolation room. With one swipe, I cut through his uniform, deep into his forearm.

He winced, but didn't let go. Instead, he pulled me against a wall.

"Drop that."

Yeah, right.

I lunged at him again, but he easily caught my arm and slammed it against the wall. I cried out.

He did it one more time and my hand opened, dropping the piece of glass. He bent over, still holding on to me, and picked it up.

"Interesting."

I said nothing.

He looked up, catching my eyes in his.

Again, he pulled me through one corridor after another, until he brought us to a stop in front of a door, one of the many that lined that particular hallway. Flinging it open, he pushed me inside.

"Now," he said, "if you'd stop behaving like a wildcat, I'd like to know why every time I see you, you're at the business end of a rifle."

He crossed the room to a large desk pressed against an even larger window. Opening one of the glistening drawers, he pulled out a bottle of alcohol and a bit of gauze.

Since I'd remained quiet, he looked up again. "Well?"

"Screw you."

He stared at me with such intensity I had to force myself not to look away. "Aren't you afraid of anything?"

I blinked. "Nothing that you can do to me."

"Really?"

Captain Summers wiped at the gash on his forearm, pouring the alcohol straight into the wound. I couldn't help flinching.

"See, that ruins some of the fun, because as we walked here, I was thinking of what punishment would be suitable. When I wasn't concentrating on keeping you from stabbing me, that is. But, I suppose, if you're not scared, then I don't see the point." He dabbed at the gash in his arm with a piece of gauze. "I had been thinking along the lines of pulling your fingernails off one by one." He lifted his eyes to me then lowered them back to his arm. "Perhaps electroshock. Or maybe a few days in the isolation room."

I was suddenly cold, my stomach twisting in knots.

He cocked his head as he watched me. "So that's it, then."

He smiled through the transparent mask. I didn't know why I noticed, but the smile, slightly crooked, suited his angular face. "Unfortunately, the isolation room is being used at the moment, and we can't really stick two people in there. Kind of misses the point. So," he ripped the gauze with his hands and wound the end around his arm, "there's not much else I can do, punishment-wise."

"Why am I here, then?"

"You could show a little gratitude, you know. If I'd left you there with the guards, your brains would have been all over the floor by now."

"I'm not going to thank you."

He sighed and walked closer to me. "I've been hearing a lot about you, Maya, from the other guards. You seem to be constantly in the middle of trouble."

I opened my mouth to tell him that most of it wasn't my fault, that other people had started the majority of the issues, but it seemed like a stupid thing to say. I wasn't going to act like a whiny kid. Not with this man.

I held his gaze as he waited for me to say something.

"You have nothing to say to that?"

"No."

"Okay." He turned around, heading for one of the two armchairs in the room, and sat down on an armrest. "How's…uh…the kid you rescued?"

"He's fine."

"What's his name again?"

Damn. The less he knew about him, the better. "Tom."

The Captain nodded. He smiled again.

It really was a pleasant smile. I leapt back from that thought. *Do not go there.*

"One more question," he said. "Do you know how to use computers?"

The change in subject, not only in the conversation, but inside my own head, made me pause. Besides, didn't everyone know how to use computers?

I hesitated. "Yeah. I can't design a webpage or anything, but basic stuff, of course."

"Good. Okay, Maya. I think we're done here. Do you think you'll be able to avoid getting yourself killed for the rest of the day?"

"I can try. No promises, though."

To my surprise, he actually laughed. It filled the room with bright sound.

"Fair enough. Oh, I'm keeping this, by the way," he said, lifting my piece of glass. All the laughter suddenly drained out of his eyes and I was back in the room with someone who could have me killed with a couple of words.

He brought a cell phone out of his pocket and pressed a button. "Come take the girl back to work," he said to whoever picked up on the other end. With his free hand, he tossed the piece of bloodied glass into the air, catching it without effort.

He was still flinging it when a guard stepped into the room to take me back.

"Have a good night, Maya," he said.

I turned around with a snort and followed the guard out.

* * * *

Jessica and Tom were waiting for me in the main hall.

"I thought that guy was going to put you in the isolation room again," Jessica said, wrapping her arms around me.

"No, apparently, there's someone in there already. Lucky me."

While I was gone, Tom had found out from one of the girls assigned to bathroom duties that Lesley had torn her throat open.

"She bled out in seconds," he said. It was supposed to be comforting to know it'd been a quick death, but it wasn't. What had she felt in those last seconds? What kind of pain had she suffered through?

"I don't understand why they all do that, the tearing," Jessica said.

"I don't know. Maybe they feel like they're suffocating."

"Yeah, but what about the ones who go for their arms? My dad ripped his stomach open. Why would he do that if he couldn't breathe?" Tom said.

I sighed. If the doctors hadn't been able to figure it out yet, the three of us didn't stand a chance.

The day passed slowly. I hadn't noticed until now how much a part of our group Lesley had been. Despite her sarcasm, her dryness, or maybe because of them, she kept us firmly in the present, not allowing our heads to get away from us. Now it felt like there was nothing to ground us. No one to point out the way things really were.

When the lights went off, I pulled the blanket over Tom and me. Without a word, he moved close enough so that our shoulders touched. It was a simple gesture, just letting me know that he was there, but it meant much more than anything he could have said.

* * * *

Another person collapsed during roll call the next morning and was dragged out. He hadn't even been that sick, so I figured he'd been too weak to stand for too long.

As always, I peered past the fence while I waited for my name, towards the adult's part of the courtyard, but I didn't expect to see Mom. If she was still alive, she'd be as unrecognizable by now as I was.

Captain Summers was standing closer to Mole Man than usual. He looked around as the names were called, catching my eyes a few times and holding my gaze for a second or two before moving on.

"Maya Salaise," Mole Man finally said.

"Here."

"You'll be reporting to Captain Summers today."

I frowned. What the hell was this about now? I rifled through the previous day, trying to find anything I might have said or done to get myself into new trouble. I came up empty. Well, except for stabbing him and telling him to go screw himself.

When the names ran out and people started walking to their jobs, I looked over at the Captain, who barely motioned to me with a slight nod of his head.

"Be careful," Tom said. "Don't get yourself in trouble."

"Why does everyone keep telling me that?"

He rolled his eyes. "Yeah, I wonder."

The Captain's eyes were void of expression when I stepped up to him. They moved from me to Tom and back, registering something I couldn't read.

He didn't speak as he led us once again down the many hallways to the same room I'd been in yesterday. Now, though, instead of the two bulky armchairs, the room had another desk with a computer perched on top of it.

He closed the door and finally spoke. "I need someone to type letters and memos and things like that. Think you can handle it?"

"A five year old could handle it."

"Great, then it should be no trouble for you." He nodded towards the desk. "I've already left three letters that need to be typed. Once you're done, make a file for them and I'll send them out. I'd have you do it, but it is not a good idea for you to use the Internet."

"Fine."

I walked around the desk. The computer was one of those massive ones, a war horse with a thick armature, a yellowing white structure. I was surprised it still worked, since it couldn't be younger than a decade.

Lifting my hand to the power button, I suddenly paused. "You do know I'm sick, right? I'm going to be touching this thing with my 'diseased' hands."

Captain Summers smiled. "Of course. But I ordered this computer for your own private use. When I send the emails out, I'll make sure to wear gloves."

I shrugged. "Whatever you say."

I scooted my chair closer and forced myself to concentrate on the paper in front of me. I started typing. Or tried to, since his writing was close to illegible. He had a sloping handwriting that was as sharp as his features, making blades of consonants on the page.

Captain Summers sat at his own desk, reading over folders packed with papers, his gaze so concentrated on the words in front of him, he didn't notice the few times I glanced over at him. Like that, he looked more like a college student studying for an exam than a Captain.

I pulled my eyes away and back to the handwriting.

Around mid-morning, a woman came in with a small tray. She paused when she saw me.

"Leave it right on the desk, Jill. Thanks," Captain Summers said.

The woman, Jill, did as she was told and left, but not without first looking at me as if I were covered in cockroaches.

I rolled my eyes.

"I really don't know how to make it clearer to them," Captain Summers suddenly said. "I don't drink tea, and I especially don't drink tea with milk." He sighed and sat back in his chair. He looked over at me, making me drop my gaze to the keyboard.

From the corner of my eye, I saw him get up, lift the tray, and walk over to where I was.

"Do you like tea?"

I frowned. Was he really offering me his breakfast?

"It's not a trick question, Maya. I'm not going to pour it over your head or anything."

I nodded. "Yes. I like tea."

"Good." He lowered the tray onto the desk.

I hesitated, looking from the cup to him.

A slight crease rose on his forehead. "It's not poisoned. That would be a strange thing for me to do, don't you think? Look." He lifted the cup to his lips and took a sip. "See? It's perfectly fine, though too sweet for my taste." Gently, he lowered the cup, then walked back to his desk.

Despite his demonstration, it took me a few seconds to make up my mind if I really should drink it. He was the enemy. One of the people who'd set this place up and brought us all here. I shouldn't accept charity from him.

But my throat ached, my chest rumbled with a cough that had already started to get worse, and the tea smelled too good. With trembling hands I reached out and brought the warm cup to my own lips.

It was sweet, and thick with cream, not milk. My mouth came alive with the sweetness, with the heat, and in less than a minute I'd drunk the whole thing.

When I looked up, the Captain's eyes were on me, taking in my every movement. He didn't look away and neither did I.

"I'm not going to thank you," I said.

He nodded once and picked up one of his files again.

* * * *

"I don't understand what he wants with you," Jessica said. She sipped at her broth.

"It does seem strange. Can't he just type up his own letters?" Tom said.

"That's what I've been asking myself, but I'm not complaining. I just have to sit at a desk and type." For some reason, I couldn't bring myself to mention the whole tea business. It just didn't feel right to flaunt it.

"Does he say anything important in them? You know, about what's going on outside?" Tom looked up at me, his light eyes so bright. As always, there was a small smile just waiting to bloom on his lips. After spending the day with someone who studied me like a field specimen, it was a pretty dramatic shift.

"No. It's mostly arrangements for the film crew. Nothing that really means much to us."

Tom frowned. "I've been thinking about the film crew. I don't even see the point in showing the public anything, actually. Would they even care what happens in here as long as the 'diseased' stay far away from them?"

He was right. No one had put up any kind of struggle when the new ambulances started taking people away, no one had even asked too much about it, as if the less they knew the better, the safer they were. Why would they care now?

As I was about to say all of this, a young girl came into the main hall. I'd never seen her before.

She looked around, fright making her already thin face appear thinner. Almost immediately behind her came a boy, this one older.

The girl who kept track of everyone with her chalk marks hurried to take up her position next to the wall.

"What's going on?" Jessica asked.

In their corner, Elize and her group sat up straighter, their eyes locked on the door. Dawn said something to Kyle, who laughed.

"I think it's a new group of people." I stood up, the pain in my chest gripping hold of me tightly and propelling me into a cough.

Tom also stood and grabbed my hand.

The spasm worked its way through me, then died.

"Wave them over," I said when I could speak, my voice harsh from coughing. "Keep them away from those three."

Tom lifted his hand and called to them. "Over here!"

The girl and boy looked up and immediately started walking towards us. I frowned. They were so trusting. Had I been like that?

"Hi," I said when they were in front of us. I caught Elize looking over, a thin smile on her lips. I twirled my fingers at her and she looked away.

"Hi," the oldest girl said. "Where are we?"

"You're in Levelry, one of those centers people talked about." Jessica smiled at them, trying to ease the transition. I couldn't bring myself to do it. I couldn't just pretend this place was anything but what it was: a prison, a death camp.

More people came in, kids and teens, no one younger than twelve, still leaving Sophia the youngest in the main hall. I didn't even want to consider what was happening to the toddlers and the babies who were sick or who had parents who were sick. If I allowed myself to think about it, I was afraid of losing everything that was holding me together.

The three of us explained the basics of how Levelry worked to the ones who came over to the corner. Not all of them did, though, especially some of the older ones, the ones our age.

I saw the kids' expressions tighten when I told them there would be no more food for tonight and I cringed, thinking of how hungry I'd been that first day. But there was nothing we could do.

Tom looked over at one guy, Jake, someone who'd be finishing high school in a few months if he hadn't gotten sick. "What's going on out there?"

Jake shrugged. "Things are worse. There are more centers now, one practically in every state. More people are disappearing, too. And not all of them are sick."

The increase in centers explained why we hadn't seen any new people arrive before now.

A girl, Sarah, nodded. "One of my neighbors called the cops on another neighbor because their dog barked too much. She told them the entire household was sick."

Tom, Jessica, and I looked at each other. It sounded like something out of a movie, not something that could be happening in our country.

"There have been rumors," Jake said, "that these places weren't 'health centers' or whatever, but the majority of people don't pay attention to them. They just want the sick people far away from them."

I thought of Lisa and Martin. Of Derek. Had they been taken to centers? And if they had, had they survived?

"It's funny," Jake said, "because the President went on TV the other day and actually said the number of sick people had lowered." He snorted. "Yeah, because half the country is locked up."

"Then that's why they want to bring the camera crew in here. To calm people down. To squash whatever rumors are going around," I said.

Tom nodded. "The last thing the government wants is a riot on their hands."

"Yeah," Sarah said.

I bit my lip. If things outside were as bad as what they were saying, then, whether the government wanted it or not, something had to change.

The question was if we could do anything about it from in here.

* * * *

I was walking back from the bathroom before lights out when I saw Elize leaning against one of the walls nearby. She was supposed to be back in the main hall. I'd waited to use the bathroom until now so that I wouldn't bump into her. They hadn't bothered me in days, but it was better to avoid them altogether.

When I saw her smile, I knew I was in trouble. My hands went immediately to my waistband before I remembered I no longer had the piece of glass tucked in there.

"I heard down the grapevine that you are back to being your defenseless, pathetic self." She walked forward and stopped. I heard footsteps behind me and whirled around. Of course, it was Kyle and Dawn.

"Leave me alone," I said.

"Yeah, I don't think so."

"What the hell do you have against me, Elize? I didn't do anything to you."

She smiled again. "I don't know. There's just something about you."

Kyle grabbed my right arm, twisting it behind me. I was getting ready to scream, hoping to surprise them, when Dawn's hand wrapped around my mouth, muffling the sound.

A rain of pain fell on me. Elize kicked me until my legs gave way, then they took turns. The rage on their faces made them unrecognizable, distorting them until they didn't even look human anymore.

When I saw their expressions, I finally understood the truth behind their attacks. The fury at the circumstance we were all in, at the lack of hope and basic rights we all deserved, they melded together into the hate on their three faces.

Their minds had been twisted by this place. Whoever they'd really been before all of this had died when the buses dropped them here.

I struggled, trying to kick them away, but all that did was make them hit harder, until I thought for sure they'd kill me.

Time passed, probably just a couple of minutes that stretched into an eternity. Finally they stopped.

I waited until I couldn't hear them anymore before attempting to sit up. Everything hurt; every part of my body had been kicked or punched. Crawling to the nearest wall, I used it to pull myself up into a sort of hunched, standing position. My legs and stomach had received the worst of it, but I didn't think anything was broken. The pain was bad but not that bad.

"Maya?" Tom's voice came from around the corner.

"Tom, I'm here."

His clear eyes widened when he saw me. "Jesus, what happened? Who did this?"

"It doesn't matter."

"Of course it matters. It was those three, right?"

"Forget it. Just help me."

He hurried to my side, wrapping his arm around me, propping me up. I groaned as I tried to straighten.

"I'll carry you," he said.

"No. I'll look too weak."

He pulled me closer, taking more of my weight on his body. Despite his own illness, he felt strong, his muscles taut beneath his tunic. We started inching our way back to the main hall.

"We have to do something," he said.

"What? The guards don't care." I winced. "Let's stop for a second."

Tom held me up carefully. I looked up at his face, creased with concern, and gave him a small smile. "You look better."

He blinked. "Yeah, can't really say the same about you."

I laughed, the adrenaline that had moved through my body during the attack pouring out in my laughter. "I'm such a mess," I said when I could breathe again.

"Yes. But you look lovely anyway."

I looked up at him, really feeling his nearness for the first time. I cleared my throat almost shyly. "Okay, we can try again."

Slowly, we made it back to the main hall, where I'd just managed to collapse on the floor before the lights went off.

Chapter Sixteen

Captain Summers' eyebrows rose when I stepped into his office the following morning.

I'd woken with deep, dark bruises the color of eggplants all over my body, including on one of my cheeks where Dawn had landed a punch.

He watched me as I moved carefully to my desk, flinching as I lowered myself into the chair.

"What happened?"

I turned the computer on. "Nothing."

He dropped the papers he'd been reading. "Right. You just woke up with a bruise on your face and pain bad enough you can barely walk."

"It's none of your business," I said, my voice tight with anger. They could keep me locked up, keep me sick and half-starved, but they would not get inside my head.

"Yes, it is. You are all my business."

"Then you should pay closer attention to what happens to us." I grabbed the first sheet of paper, half full with his handwriting and started typing.

I gathered all my attention and tried to focus it on the task in front of me so that it might distract me from the aches in my body.

We worked in silence for a while, although, by the lack of movement and sound from his desk, I doubted he was doing anything but watching me.

Finally, when I was about to say something that might have landed me in the isolation room again, he stood and walked the few steps to my desk.

From his jacket pocket he brought out the piece of glass he'd taken from me. I looked up at his face. Why had he kept it?

"Here," he said, holding it out to me.

"You're giving me a weapon?"

His face had no expression. "Are you planning on cutting me with it again?"

"Not right now."

His lips twitched with what I thought was a smile.

Still watching him, I reached out and grabbed the piece of glass. It was still warm from his uniform.

I opened my mouth.

"Yeah, I know. You're not going to thank me," he said, cocking an eyebrow.

I shook my head.

"All is as it should be, then." He turned around and went back to his desk.

Three days passed. My bruises lightened, though some of them were still sore, and I was able to walk again without limping.

I made sure to let Elize and her minions know I was once again armed by going so far as sneaking behind her in the food line and pressing my glass shard into her back. I felt her skin tear beneath the weapon's tip.

"Leave me alone, Elize. I mean it," I'd said.

And so far, she seemed to be listening.

Captain Summers hadn't talked about the bruises any more in the last three days. He actually hadn't said much at all, though every morning he passed me the tea with cream the woman brought in. It was strange, but I didn't question it.

Every once in a while I felt his gaze on me and would turn to find him watching me work, his hands resting on the papers he'd been reading. It was peculiar, but I couldn't blame him. The pages he gave me to type were beyond dull, so whatever he was reading couldn't be much better.

Every slip of paper that passed through my hands was more boring than the last. Until today.

I frowned at the words in front of me.

"Sergeant, in answer to your email, yes, I do believe Levelry, as one of the centers first constructed, is also one of the ones in worst condition. There is so much to do to clean it up for the cameras that I require as much help as possible. Sir, if you could send more officers, it would be a tremendous help."

My hands paused on the keyboard. That was just what we needed, more officers wielding their power like machetes.

"Something bothering you?" Captain Summers said from his desk.

Damn, he'd been watching me again. What was it with him and the staring?

"We don't need more officers," I said, blurting the words out before I could stop myself.

"You're not supposed to read the letters."

I glanced over at him. He was, like the last few days, reading through piles of papers and files, things with charts and graphs that looked boring enough to put an insomniac to sleep.

"If you know of a way to type without actually reading, then let me know."

His eyebrows came up, his eyes brightening just a bit. He smiled at me. With a sigh, he leaned back in his chair. "So what's wrong with more officers?"

"The guards are assholes. They actually bet on how long some of us will live. There's no way that adding more of them will bring anything but extra problems."

He tapped the desk with his fingers. "So what do you suggest?"

I looked away, finding his gaze too strong. I could almost feel it on my skin. "There are some basic things we need. Blankets for everyone, and I mean everyone, not just those who are there to grab them first."

"I thought everyone already had blankets."

Glancing up, I saw the frown on his forehead. He hadn't known how bad things really were?

"And food, we need better quality and more of it. Weak broth and a slice of bread is not enough for anyone, especially the children."

The Captain ran a hand through his hair, making me notice he had taken his gloves off. They were on the desk, folded together and forgotten.

"I'm not supposed to babysit you all, you know. I just have to keep as many of you alive as I can."

I gritted my teeth. "Well, if you really want to do that, then we need these things. And if you bring cameras in here and actually plan on having what they film make a difference in the public's opinion, then you'll have to 'babysit' us."

He was about to say something when a spasm gripped my chest. I tried to stop the cough from rising, but it was impossible.

I covered my mouth and twisted in the midst of the spell. Something popped in the back of my throat and I could feel the coppery taste of blood on my tongue.

I was so focused on the pain that I didn't see him stand up and come around his desk to where I was struggling. His hands came to my body and held my shoulders back, when all they wanted to do was hunch over and give into the cough.

Slowly, the spasm passed.

"Our instinct is to bend over, but it's actually better to keep your back straight," he said. His voice was no louder than a murmur. "It's easier for the air to find its way in."

I breathed in deeply, filling my aching lungs, Captain Summers' hands a warm, firm pressure on my back.

"Better?"

I nodded.

He removed his hands and came around to face me. "How long have you had the cough?"

I cleared my throat and managed to find my voice. "A couple of days."

The Captain lifted a hand again, his fingers long and almost translucent, and brought it close to me. I flinched and he paused.

"I'm not going to hurt you," he said.

As gently as a caress of air, he placed the back of his hand against my forehead. The touch set my skin tingling in an alarming way.

"You've got a fever."

"I've had one since I've been here."

He didn't remove his hand yet, instead turning it over so the tips of his finger brushed my hairline.

When a shiver ran down my back, I shifted, moving my head away. "You don't have your gloves on," I said.

He swallowed and took a step back. "And you are so very worried that I'll get sick."

"I don't want anyone to catch this from me." My heart was beating so quickly, as if I'd just finished a swim match. What had just happened here?

He put a hand in one of his pockets and brought out a bottle of aspirin. "This might help the fever."

I nodded and took the bottle from his hand, making sure we didn't touch.

He glanced at me one more time and left the room.

* * * *

It took a smaller action, though, to untangle the confusion I felt in Captain Summer's presence.

We were walking to roll call one of those interchangeable mornings, Tom beside me and Jessica trying to talk in between yawns in front of us, when we heard something hit the cement floor. Except it wasn't something, but someone.

Tom looked over some of the people near us. "I think it's Sophia."

"Is she okay?" I asked.

"I can't see from here."

We tried to move closer, but the trio of teens in front of us made no room.

"Do you mind?" Tom said to three guys, motioning for them to get out of the way.

The teens looked at him as if he spoke in another language then turned back around. I shook my head. This was ridiculous.

"Hey," I said. "Get the hell out of the way." Maybe rudeness would work better.

With an exaggerated roll of the eyes, one of the guys moved to the side, just enough for me to slip through.

It was Sophia. She'd tripped, it seemed, and was having trouble getting back up. Another girl, the one who did the chalk marks on the wall, was trying to help her to her feet, but Sophia's small hands kept pushing her away.

There was a shout from the guards from out in the courtyard. Apparently we were a tad late for roll call. People started to hurry.

The chalk girl gave me a quick look as I walked towards her and Sophia and shrugged.

"Go," I said. "We'll help her."

She nodded and left.

"Sophia, you okay?" Jessica said, hurrying to my side.

"I fell."

"Did you hurt anything?"

"No."

Still, I tested her knees, her arms and her legs, but everything seemed to be all right.

"You all need to get to the courtyard."

My head whipped up at the voice. Captain Summers was standing at the door leading outside.

"If they start calling names before you're there, you'll be in serious trouble." His eyes traveled to all of us, coming to rest on me last. "I'll take her."

I felt Tom tighten next to me. "We can do it."

"It's all right. Really." Captain Summers looked at me. "I'll make sure she's there when her name is called. Right, Sophia?"

I blinked. How did he know her name?

The guard outside shouted the last warning. We had to go.

Captain Summers knelt and placed his gloved hands under Sophia's arms. He gently helped her to her feet. "Go," he said to us.

"Come on." I grabbed Jessica's arm. Tom was still watching Sophia, his face tight with anger. "Tom, let's go." I took his hand and pulled him out with us into the courtyard.

But it wasn't any of that that truly left an imprint on me. No, that came moments later.

Captain Summers did as he'd promised and brought Sophia out before the guards called her name. He had a hand on her shoulder as he led her to the line.

There was absolute silence from the other guards, but their disapproval was visible in their hard stares. This was obviously something he shouldn't be doing.

As the Captain left Sophia's side, it happened. For a moment, so quickly I could have missed it if I'd blinked, he pressed his hand against her cheek. It was such a gentle touch, like a brother would give his sister for comfort, that it shook me. I felt as if everything inside me had been flipped upside down.

I turned away, feeling my cheeks grow hot with this new sensation. It was foreign, and not welcomed, but it was there. What was I supposed to do now?

"Everything okay?" Tom whispered next to me.

I nodded. But no. Things were definitely not okay.

* * * *

I did my best to avoid his eyes all of that morning and afternoon, but it didn't help as much as I would have liked.

"You're very quiet today," he said.

"Am I?" I kept my eyes on the keyboard in front of me, although I hadn't really been paying any attention to what I'd been writing. I guessed I had found a way of typing without actually reading.

"You're not mumbling as you type."

I frowned. "I don't mumble."

"Yes, actually, you do. You say the words to yourself as you type them."

"That's ridiculous. I would have realized if I did that."

"I'll have to record you, then, for you to believe me."

I glanced up, catching his smile. Great.

"You must be distracted today, then," he said.

I sighed. Might as well ask what I'd been wondering. "How did you know Sophia's name?"

He cocked his head to the side. "I stand out there practically every day with all of you. I know your names."

"You didn't know mine."

"No, but I was out of Levelry for a week or two after your group came in. I came back that night the guards dragged you out to shoot you. Just in time."

"Yeah, except you did almost let them shoot me."

He was silent for a moment, looking back down at his hands. "I wasn't going to allow them to do it, Maya. I just needed to see something."

I frowned. "What?"

"I needed to see if they would. And I got my answer."

I snorted. Had he really not realized what went on in this place? "They do it all the time. It's a game to them."

"Yes, I know that now." He looked as if he wanted to say something else, but he just cleared his throat and went back to his papers.

And all I could think, as I lowered my eyes, was how much I wanted to hear what he had to say.

V.C. REPETTO

Chapter Seventeen

I breathed with relief as I walked back to the main hall. The day was finally over. It had been almost a week of avoiding glances and trying to keep my thoughts on the pages in front of me and not on the young man sitting in the same room with me.

I knew there was something wrong as soon as I neared the main hall. The noise was less than usual, even in the line of people waiting for food.

Tom was right by the door and he seemed to have been waiting for me.

"What's the matter?" I said.

"It's Sophia. She collapsed during work."

"Is it the last stage?"

Tom shook his head. "No. She just fainted. Jessica and I managed to keep her hidden from the guards."

I started to follow him in but he stopped me. "Get your food first, otherwise they'll think something's going on."

I did so, as quickly as I could, then walked inside, swallowing the broth in the seconds it took to get from the line to where Tom and Jessica were.

Sophia was wrapped in a blanket, with another one shaped into a pillow under her head. I hadn't seen her close up like this in a few days and I had to dig my nails into my palms to keep from gasping.

She looked like something out of a horror movie. Her jaw-line and cheekbones were doing their best to slice through her skin, which was thin and translucent enough for me to see the web of veins beneath it. Her breathing was shallow and forceful, with a whistle behind every breath.

She looked like she was starving.

"We gave her sips of broth and water, but it made no difference," Jessica said.

No, it was too late now. I sat down, tucking my legs beneath me. "I didn't know she was this weak." I took her hand. It was cold and damp.

We stayed by her, in silence, watching as she struggled for air until the lights were turned off.

"Go to sleep. I'll wake you if anything changes," Tom said in the darkness.

"No, it's all right. I'm not tired." I didn't think I could close my eyes even if I tried. "You sleep, Tom."

I could tell he wanted to say something else, maybe even sit up with me, but I turned away and hoped he'd get the message. He did.

The groans and whispers slowly died out as I sat with Sophia until the room was as quiet as it ever got.

I wished I had something to say to her, something that might comfort her if she could hear me wherever she was. But all the words dried on my tongue, turning to ash. I couldn't even mention Toby. I didn't know if I'd be able to lie now. So I just held her hand and waited for her heart to give up or for morning to come. Either way, she wouldn't survive.

Quiet footsteps came around to where I was sitting an hour or two later.

"You should do the right thing."

It was Elize's voice.

"What?"

"You know what I'm talking about," she whispered. "You have a way of ending this for her. She's completely out of it, so she wouldn't feel the cut and she'd die in her sleep. In a few minutes."

My eyes widened in the dark. "You're suggesting I kill her? Are you nuts?"

"You prefer to watch her slowly starve to death?"

"Funny thing to say, coming from you."

"That was different. We didn't have much choice but to do what the guards said."

I snorted. "Yeah, but you seemed to really enjoy it." I gripped Sophia's hand tighter. "Just go back to sleep, Elize."

She was silent for a moment. "You're a coward," she said and walked back to her spot.

Her words stayed with me long after she had stopped moving.

A coward.

And she didn't even know that I had an almost full bottle of aspirin inside one of my slippers. I didn't have to use the piece of glass; I could just give Sophia the pills, stick them down her throat, and force her to swallow. How many would she need, ten, twelve, to allow her to drift away in her sleep?

But I couldn't do it. There was no way.

Maybe Elize was right. What was so courageous about fighting for your own life? Everyone here was doing it; animals did it constantly, it was just instinct. Even helping Tom could have been seen as a way of avoiding any feelings of guilt at seeing him so defenseless and doing nothing about it. But now that I was asked to do something solely for someone else, to make a choice that would make another person's last moments easier, I flinched away as if I'd been burned.

Sophia coughed. Even that sounded weak.

I leaned forward. "I'm sorry, Sophia. I really am."

V.C. REPETTO

* * * *

The guards shot her the following morning.

Chapter Eighteen

I didn't cry, as I had not really cried for Lesley. I think somewhere in me I understood that if I started crying I would not know how to stop.

I worked instead. I filled the hours and my thoughts with the Captain's words, even hearing the cadence in which he would say them. It kept me busy and I was glad for it. If I'd had a repetitive, mindless task like weeding or sweeping, I would have cracked into little pieces.

Three days after Sophia's death, I found the file.

Captain Summers had spent very little time in the office the previous couple of days, only stopping by every few hours to pick up papers. One time he stepped into the room, stopped to fuss with a drawer, and left without saying anything. I didn't know if he'd heard of Sophia's death, thought I doubted it. No one would report every single death to him.

But even if he didn't know, he had surprised me by doing what I'd suggested. Before lights out yesterday we'd each been passed a blanket by the guards, and our broth had actual pieces of meat in it.

"This is strange," Jessica said. "To be given these things all of the sudden."

I said nothing, but when I lifted my eyes from my bowl of broth I caught Tom watching me. I smiled and he returned it, though it wasn't as bright as his smiles usually were.

"It's probably for the whole TV thing," I said.

They both nodded, but I knew Tom wasn't convinced.

I didn't know why I was so hesitant to speak of the time I spent in the Captain's office. It was ridiculous. Which is why I was glad when he started spending time outside his office doing whatever it was he did.

This morning, I'd finished the two letters he'd left for me in record time. His handwriting was becoming familiar and I no longer needed a decoder ring to figure out the most basic of sentences. I didn't want to admit it to myself, but I'd grown to like the sharp strokes that marked a "t" or a "y". They were almost pleasant to look at.

So with nothing to do until lunch, I started poking around the computer. I had Internet access but it was password protected, so instead I turned to the many, many folders spread across the desktop.

I went one by one, finding lists of supplies, maps, coordinates I couldn't understand, just lots of information that was completely useless to me.

Until I saw the file marked "Levelry Living Inventory". My stomach twisted. Could this be a list of the people alive here?

I double clicked on it and a rectangle to input a password came up on the screen. Behind it I saw the Internet logo. So the file was connected to the network, probably to keep it updated as people came in or died.

Damn it.

My fingers hovered over the keys. The password could have been anything. I tried all the common ones, numbers in order, the word "password", even "qwerty", but none of them worked. I really hadn't expected it to be that easy but I was still disappointed.

Sighing, I sat back. I lifted my eyes and almost screamed when I saw Captain Summers standing in the doorway.

"A bit jumpy today," he said. His eyes shifted from me, as if they didn't want to spend too much time looking my way. "I wonder why."

He came into the room and walked behind me, standing much closer than was necessary. For the first time, I noticed his scent, a mixture of creamy soap and crisp aftershave. Too late I realized I shouldn't have noticed that.

My heart pounded as he bent down so his head was right next to mine. His eyes were on the screen, on the blank rectangle blinking in front of us.

"I see," he said.

With a swift move, his hands came up to the keyboard, his fingers dancing over the keys, not bothering to hide the password. It was just a name: "Tatiana."

The computer beeped and the screen changed to a list.

"You should have asked me," he said. "I would have opened it for you."

I swallowed. "You weren't here."

My voice sounded so small. Why did he have this effect on me, when none of the other guards, not even Elize and her group, made me feel this shaky anymore?

"True. Well, go on."

I put my hand back on the mouse and started scrolling. Like I'd thought, it was a list of everyone alive in Levelry, organized by arrival date. The first names had arrived months ago, when the epidemic had first started.

When had Mom and I gotten here? It felt like it'd been years, but it couldn't be more than a month and a half, maybe two.

I kept scrolling, my eyes following the names and dates down to the moment the nightmare had started for us. Next to me, I was aware of Captain Summers' breathing, his slight shifts as he glanced from me to the screen and back.

Suddenly, there was my name. My eyes jumped down a row. Mom wasn't there. I held my breath so I wouldn't scream.

"It can't be right," I whispered. "They must have skipped her name." Everything in me knew this was nonsense, but I couldn't allow myself to think the truth, that my mom had died.

Without a word, Captain Summers placed his hand on top of mine. Slowly, he guided the mouse to another file, one marked "Deceased" and double clicked it, pressing gently down on my fingers. Another list of names came on the screen, blurred by the tears already filling my eyes.

He scrolled down the page, still keeping my hand trapped under his warm pressure. He stopped.

There, many, many lines down from the top, was Mom's name.

"I'm sorry, Maya," he whispered.

Tears trickled silently down my face. Another death. Another person I loved taken by this place. I closed my eyes and held my breath, trying to control the violence bubbling in my stomach. If I let it, it'd take over me.

"I can find out how, if you'd like," he said.

I blinked, turning my head to face him. He looked so young. "Why would you do that? Why do you even care?"

His eyes lost their hard quality for an instant as they watched me. "I don't know."

The words dug into me. I removed my hand from under his and turned away.

"Yes, I want to know how she died."

He nodded."Done."

* * * *

His hands were on me, gentle as feathers but with a strength lurking just beneath the surface that pulled at me. His face was in darkness, was of darkness, so that all I could see were his fingers, his palms, then slowly, as light trailed up his body, what looked like numbers in ink appeared. The more I looked, though, the more they twisted, opening up, becoming a bleeding wound.

I woke with a gasp.

My tunic was clinging to my sweat-covered skin. I tried to catch my breath, but I kept gasping, unable to get the air I needed.

I rubbed my eyes, which were still swollen from the bout of crying that had overtaken me from the moment the lights went out until I'd fallen asleep.

Captain Summers had disappeared for the rest of the afternoon, only coming back to give me the promised answer. He hadn't hesitated, but said the one word I'd feared most to hear.

"Starvation," he said. "She died three weeks after you both arrived."

I'd felt nothing at first. Shock seemed to grant me an instant of peace, short-lived, but powerful.

I just looked at him, his eyes as dark and hard as they always were, holding his gaze, and feeling the strength behind it bolstering me up. I wouldn't break down, not there in front of him, and he seemed to understand it.

"Go," he said, stepping away from the door.

Tom and Jessica had said the appropriate words, gathering around me to make sure no one bothered me.

When Elize had made the faintest attempt at a joke at my expense, Tom had crossed the room in three bounds and said something I couldn't hear but which actually made her flinch. At any other time, it would have been thrilling to see her frightened.

But grief had burrowed inside me already.

She'd starved to death. Like Sophia. Would it have been easier, though, if the Tearings had taken her and swallowed her up instead? I'd cried until I had nothing left.

My mind was now a raw wound and everything, every little thought, made it bleed. Looking around the dark room, hearing Tom shift in his sleep, and the many coughs and groans that made up our nights, I knew I'd not be able to sleep anymore.

My head throbbed as I got to my feet. The dream I'd woken from clung to me more than other dreams, refusing to let go. It wanted me to examine it, but I shrank from it. I wanted nothing to do with it.

My foot bumped into someone in the dark. There were so many new people spread around that there was little room to walk. All these people, children, teens, all of us who should have been in our own beds dreading the next school day. Would we ever set foot outside again?

Suddenly, I knew that was what I needed: to be out in the fresh night air. The room's staleness was suffocating me.

I stepped as carefully and as quickly as I could to the door that led to the hallway. I pulled, already knowing it was pointless. They never left the door unlocked, and tonight was no different.

For the first time since the day I'd arrived here, I took real stock of the boarded up windows around the room. I crossed to the nearest one and grabbed on to the edge of the wooden plank that barred the moonlight. It was just a wooden panel, held to the wall with nails that had been rusted black.

Sticking my fingers beneath the board, I pulled. It shifted under my hands a bit, but it didn't come off.

A moan left my mouth. I wanted air.

Again, I pulled, rattling the wood. "Please," I whispered. I repeated it over and over, my voice growing louder with each failed effort until the people around me started moving in their interrupted sleep.

"Maya, what are you doing?" Tom said, suddenly beside me. I hadn't heard his steps.

"I want fresh air, Tom. I can't stand it in here anymore." I heard the strain in my words, the sharp despair clinging to me.

"Maya." His hand pressed down on my shoulder, an insubstantial weight. Not nearly strong enough to yank me back from the precipice I was poised over.

"I need it, Tom." Again, I pulled on the board. My left hand slipped and the wood's edge sliced right into my palm. "Shit!" I screamed. I made my hands into fists, ignoring the blood already pooling in my injured hand, and pounded on the wooden board.

"Stop," Tom said. His hands grabbed onto my wrists and pulled. "Maya, stop. You're hurting yourself."

I kicked out without a clear idea of what I wanted to hit; I just wanted to make something hurt, to crush it with my feet, to destroy it.

But Tom held on to me despite the kicking and the screaming, pressing my back against his chest and waiting while my overwhelming frustration worked its way out of my body.

It took a coughing spell to bring the rage to a stop. The pain in my chest had grown from a needle to a blade now. My body curled up instinctively, but I remembered Captain Summers' hands, the warmth of his touch pulling my shoulders back, cutting the spasm in two.

The hands, the Captain's hands, Tom's hands, one turning into the other in my dream. I closed my eyes.

"Breathe," Tom murmured into my ear. And I did.

My muscles unclenched, leaving me limp. I turned around and wrapped my arms around Tom.

He held me tightly as I lay my head on his shoulder. "I'm sorry," I whispered.

"There's nothing to be sorry about."

"My mom, Tom."

"I know. But there's nothing you can do, Maya."

A thought made me lift my head. "I didn't even look for your mom and dad, or Jessica's. I was so selfish. I should have looked for—"

"No. It's better like this. I'd rather not know, and I'm sure Jessica feels the same."

This made no sense to me. How could they not want to know?

"We're not like you, Maya. We're not brave."

I laughed, a sound as bitter as I felt. "Brave? If I'd been brave, I would have done something to find her and get us out. But I just sat here, more worried about Elize than helping my mother."

Tom looked at me. His hand came up to my face, touching the spot where the bruise was slowly disappearing. "You don't know," he murmured, soft enough that I almost didn't hear him.

"Know what?"

"How strong you are." He bent forward a little and brushed my cheek with his lips. His hand moved down to my waist, hesitating for a moment before he allowed it to touch me.

My skin tingled. I closed my eyes for an instant, but the dream came back to life behind my eyelids. Those other hands. That other touch.

I pulled back.

He blinked and lowered his hands. "I'm sorry."

"No. It's…I just…"

"You don't have to say anything." He smiled, though it wasn't the usual, blinding one I waited for. He didn't seem to know what to do.

I took one of his hands in mine and held it, pushing aside the confusion that rose in me as I thought of the two pairs of eyes that seemed to always follow me.

One light as crystal.

The other dark as ink.

V.C. REPETTO

Chapter Nineteen

We didn't mention what had happened that night, but it trailed after us, tinting our words to each other.

I didn't know what I felt, really. About anything or anyone.

I had the excuse, awful as it was, of having a cough that magnified by the hour, until the pain made it unbearable to stay upright. How had Lesley stood this without letting anyone really know what she was going through? I couldn't remember ever hearing her moan the way so many of the others did, the way I had to stop myself from doing so I wouldn't scare Jessica.

It was close to lights out the next day when I started to feel the burning under my skin. It started as a light itch in my arms and legs, as if I'd developed a sudden rash.

"You okay?" Tom said as I sipped my broth with one hand and scratched with the other.

"Yeah. I must have been bitten by a mosquito or something." Not that I'd seen or felt any bugs indoors apart from the odd cockroach. For having such a huge amount of people in deplorable conditions, Levelry was surprisingly vermin free. Oh, that was if you didn't count us.

"Let me see," he said.

"It's nothing. I'll put some water on my legs later."

"Let him see," Jessica said. She looked flushed. Fever was radiating off her so strongly I was surprised she wasn't seeing things yet. I thought back to my fever peak in the isolation room and shivered.

Tom lifted the fabric away from my right leg until he could see my knee. Despite our circumstances, my illness, and Mom's death, I still managed to feel embarrassed that I hadn't been able to shave my legs since I'd gotten here. A ridiculous thought, but there it was.

He frowned. "There's nothing here."

"It's not red?" I asked.

"No. Your leg is actually really pale."

I looked down. He was right. I was usually almost glow-in-the-dark white, but now my leg looked as if all the blood had drained from it. I couldn't even make out my normally prominent veins.

Tom lifted the other pant leg up. "The same thing with this one." His eyes, when they came up to my face, were flooded with fear. "Are you feeling all right?"

I opened my mouth, but a cough robbed me of words. It was the strongest spasm yet, and I felt something shift in my chest. I gasped as the itch flooded the rest of my skin, intensifying, as if someone had turned a faucet on to "hot". My skin, my muscles, my organs, everything felt as if I were standing in the center of a bonfire.

"Oh, God," I said. "It burns. God!"

I moved, but the sensation only grew.

"Tom, something's happening. I can't…"

I had the sudden realization, clear as anything I'd ever thought, that there was fire spreading through my body. Yes. That was what was wrong. Any sense of where I was disappeared.

My hands immediately started hitting my legs, trying to extinguish the flames I couldn't see but that I knew, I knew, were inside me.

My eyelids caught fire as my brain started burning. If I could just get to them, though, I could stop the pain.

Voices surrounded me, but I couldn't make out what they were saying. I didn't care; all I wanted was to stop the burning.

My arms were the worst, though. The pain was blinding, the kind that had no end, that had no borderline, that extended on into the future. I remembered the piece of glass tucked into my waistband and fumbled to get to it. I brought it out and buried it in my upper arm until my fingertips felt wet with blood. Good. A little more and I'd find the flames.

But something had my hands, both of them, holding them away from my body.

"No! Let go!" I screamed, feeling fire lap up my tongue. I pulled and tried to pry myself loose, but I couldn't. "I'm burning! Please!"

Whatever held me tightened its grip, knocking the glass out of my grasp and pinning my hands down to my sides. It held them there even when I buried my nails into its skin. Nothing would make it let me go.

And the fire rose, the burning becoming the only thing I'd ever felt and the only thing I would ever feel.

My eyes and mouth burned up, leaving me in the darkest of silences.

* * * *

I've gone blind. That was my first thought, and a rather logical one, when I opened my eyes. My eyelids were stuck to each other as if I'd spent hours crying, so that I had to tug them to open them all the way. There was only blackness around me.

"Don't move," someone said.

I knew that voice, but it was taking too long for my brain to give me the name that went with it. My muscles groaned when I moved my arms, though, so whoever it was, I'd better do as he said.

"Stay still, Maya, you're hurt."

As soon as he said it, I started to feel the soreness in my limbs and a stabbing pain on one arm, as if it had been cut open with a knife.

I remembered, then. Everything.

"I was burning."

"No. You weren't. It was the disease that made you think that."

I moaned as I tried to sit up.

"Will you stay still?" the voice said. My eyes widened as I recognized it. Captain Summers.

"I can't see."

"Neither can I," his sharp voice said. "You cried out when I tried to turn the light on."

I sighed with relief. "I'm not blind, then?"

"No."

"Can you try again?" I needed to make sure my eyes were fine. It'd felt so real, the fire, the pain.

There was a click, then a flood of light. Although it was only a small table lamp, I felt as if I were right under a spotlight, hot and impossibly bright.

I blinked and the light lost some of its extreme heat, though I still had to turn my eyes away from it.

"It just light sensitivity. I assume it'll pass."

"And if it doesn't?" I said.

"Then I'll get you some large sunglasses."

I could just make out his silhouette close to where the light radiated from. He was sitting, leaning back on a large armchair. Squinting, I looked around the room, expecting to see the Captain's office, but I didn't recognize anything in this place.

I gently moved my hands, trying to see what I was laying on. A couch of some sort, I guessed.

"What happened?" My voice was hollow-sounding, as if I'd screamed for hours, which was very probable.

The Captain stood and moved to block the light from my eyes.

My gaze flicked over to him. He didn't have the usual uniform. He was missing the jacket and gloves. He looked even younger in just his white shirt and pants.

"The disease moved on to its final stages a few hours ago. You started screaming and trying to rip your skin off. You cut yourself with that piece of glass you carried around. The guards kept it, by the way."

I swallowed. "The pain was…I really thought if I could, I don't know, get to it, I could stop it."

"Yes, which must be what everyone else thinks when they get to that point. But you were lucky." He held his gaze on me. "Your boyfriend helped you."

I frowned, feeling a twist in my stomach. "What do you mean?"

"That kid you saved, Tom whatever. He held your arms down until you passed out." He looked away. "He called one of the guards and told them you'd survived the attack. They didn't believe him, of course, but they had at least one gray cell in their combined brains to call me down to check. When I saw the tear in your arm, I knew he was telling the truth."

I looked down at my arm. It had a large, wide bandage wrapped around it, all the way up to my shoulder.

"It's a pretty serious wound," he said. "We'll have to make sure it doesn't get infected."

I remembered the panic, the slow sizzling I'd felt and shuddered.

Captain Summers walked closer, always blocking the lamp with his body. "You are the first person I've heard of who survived that stage of the disease."

"Will I get better, then?"

He shrugged. "I don't know. No one knows." He stopped moving, rubbing one hand around his other wrist. He seemed to hesitate for an instant as he closed his eyes.

As if suddenly coming to a decision, he knelt in front of the couch, so that he was at the same level as my eyes. The light burned from behind his head, making it difficult to look straight at him.

He stayed like that for a moment, watching me. Then, with a sharp movement, one of his hands came up and touched my wrist. I held my breath. His fingertips just brushed my skin, but his touch spread through me until I felt it vibrating in my body's every inch.

"I'm glad you survived," he said, his voice a murmur. His chest was rising and falling faster than it had been moments before.

The knowledge that I should pull my hand away fought against the bone-deep need to feel his skin against mine. My heart pounded.

When had this feeling started? What I was experiencing right now was not the timid nervousness, the twisting in my stomach that used to fill me when I saw Martin. It wasn't even the same calm warmth I felt with Tom.

No. This was painful. A need that turned me into pure senses. Smelling, feeling, hearing too much…wanting too much. What I felt for this young man, this person who stood for everything that had destroyed my life, was as dark as his eyes.

Those eyes now came up to my face.

"What now?" I asked.

He paused, my hand still under his fingers. "I don't know."

I took a deep breath, pushing my feelings down as far as I could hide them. "Where's Tom?"

He looked away. He slowly drew his hand back so that it no longer touched me and stood. He brought out a cell phone from his pants' pocket.

"Bring him in," he said to the person who picked up on the other end.

I forced myself to sit up, though every inch of me ached in a way I'd never felt before. I knew Captain Summers was watching me, but he didn't attempt to help me. It was a relief, since his previous touch was still thrumming on my wrist.

Seconds later, the door clicked open and a guard stepped in, Tom's arm firmly clasped in his hand.

"Thank you," said Captain Summers, dismissing the guard.

"Maya," Tom said. With a quick look towards the Captain, who was just standing there watching us, he crossed the room to the couch and wrapped his arms around me. His warmth was a comfort, like always.

"You started screaming," he said. "I did the only thing I could think of."

"Thank you," I said.

"Yes, you saved her life," said Captain Summers. He had lowered his gaze and was now inspecting the tiles beneath our feet.

A cough overtook me for a moment, straining the wound on my arm, and I clasped onto Tom as much as I could.

"Can we go back to the main hall?" he said, turning to the Captain.

"You may go, but she still needs to rest. I'll bring her down tomorrow morning."

"But—"

"Those are my orders." His voice had lost all expression.

"I'll be fine, Tom. Really."

Tom fastened his eyes on me once more.

I nodded.

He clasped me harder, then released me. "I'll see you tomorrow, then."

Captain Summers led him out to where the guard was still waiting, then stepped back into the room, closing the door behind him.

He nodded towards a door on one side of the room. "There's a bathroom there, if you'd like a shower. I'll bring another tunic for you."

I looked down at myself, at the tunic and pants splattered with bloodstains of all sizes. The sweet smell made my stomach roll with nausea.

The Captain opened the door and stepped out again.

I breathed out.

Okay, now I had to get myself up and across the room to the bathroom. Now that the light in the room had lost some of its strangeness and it no longer blinded me, I could take a good look around me.

The room had a table, a chair, and the couch I was resting on, nothing else. Not much to help me get across to the bathroom. I didn't care. If there was a hot shower waiting in there for me, then I'd crawl to get to it.

I moved one leg off the couch, the muscles slowly warming. Then the other leg.

Using the couch's armrest, I made the attempt at standing. A premature one, as it turned out.

My knees trembled then folded, bringing me down to the floor with a crunch of bone on tile. I held my breath and waited for the pain to pass.

When it did, I gripped the couch harder and despite the screaming wound on my arm, pulled myself up. I wobbled a bit, but my legs managed to hold my weight.

Slowly, I released the couch and walked up to the table, clasping it, and so on, from piece of furniture to wall, until I reached the bathroom door.

"Finally," I murmured.

I stepped inside, closing the door behind me, and turned on the light. I blinked at the brightness, a shrieking fluorescent that was sharper than the table lamp in the other room. If there'd been a window I would have left the light off, but there wasn't and I couldn't shower in the dark.

The bathroom was small, with only the shower, a toilet, and a rough piece of mirror hanging from one wall. I walked carefully to the shower. A towel hung from a ring on the wall, and though it wasn't the softest material I'd ever touched, it looked crisp and clean.

The worst part was taking the tunic off. My injured arm wouldn't turn the way I needed to get it out, so I had to use my other arm to rip the sleeve. Since the fabric was as thin as onion skin by now, this wasn't too difficult.

But the shower was glorious. How long had it been since I'd had a hot shower? All these weeks, I'd managed with the freezing trickles of water from the faucets in the bathroom, but I'd had nothing as luxurious as this.

I lifted my head, putting my face right under the spray of water, feeling its heat soaking my short hair and wiping away the blood on my skin. I could have stayed like that for hours.

Slowly, I scrubbed myself clean. The soap smelled familiar, but it took me a second to place it. I stood with it pressed against my nose until I realize it was Captain Summers' scent. I promptly dropped the bar and almost tripped on my own feet. Yeah, that would have been fun, being found unconscious and naked in the shower. In *his* shower.

I urged myself not to think about that too much and instead focus on finishing the shower without injuries.

I barely recognized my body. I hadn't seen myself naked since I'd gotten here and the change was extreme. Bones poked where before there was smooth, rounded skin; my body was just a collection of concave areas.

When my skin was red and puckered from the hot water, I stepped out and dried myself.

I knew it was a bad idea to look in the mirror, because, really, what good would it do to know what I looked like? It wasn't like I'd get out—

My thoughts cut off. The truth of what had happened tonight really landed on me. Where yesterday I'd known with complete certainty I'd never get out of Levelry alive, now things had changed. The diseases' apex had come and gone, and thanks to Tom, I was still alive.

A thought rushed through me like a cascade of cool water.

If I had made it through, who was to say there weren't other people out there who had also survived?

Surprise, fear, horror, all these things kept the majority of us from helping the person who was suffering through the last stage, but if everyone could be convinced that all it took to save their loved ones was a bit of courage and a steady grip, then we could bring all of this, the centers and the masks, the deaths, to an end.

My hands shook with excitement. That was all it would take.

Lifting my eyes, I caught my face in the mirror.

I didn't know what I'd expected but it wasn't what I saw.

My hair, though it'd been sliced off with no skill whatsoever, had started to grow in, smoothing out into a shorter version of what it'd been before. I'd always worn my hair long, but I had to admit, this cut suited me even better. It left my brown eyes as the prominent feature.

My face was thin, of course, with cheek bones that pushed into my skin, but it didn't look as morbid as I'd imagined or as I'd seen other people look. My facial structure seemed suited for starvation.

I barked out a laugh at my thoughts, followed by a string of giggles that took my breath away as much as the cough that followed it did.

"Maya, everything all right?" the Captain called out from outside the door.

Breathing deeply, I turned towards his voice. The corners of my mouth were still twitching with laughter. "Yes, I'm fine."

A beat of silence. "Open the door so I can give you the new tunic."

233

That brought the giggling to an absolute stop. Nerves, squirming and warm, took over. I clutched the towel tighter around me and grabbed the door handle.

Peeking out from the sliver of opening, I caught his eyes, eyebrows raised.

"Were you laughing in there?" he asked, handing me the fresh tunic top and pants.

I took the clothes. "Yeah."

He nodded. "An interesting sound." Clearing his throat, he turned around. "There's some food out here if you're hungry."

I put my clothes on with as much speed as I could muster, and joined him by the small table he'd dragged to the couch.

There was a sandwich on a plate in front of him and an identical one waiting for me. He was halfway through his already when I sat down.

I brought the sandwich up to my lips and noticed the ham tucked into the bread.

"Why are you smiling?"

I blinked. Had I been? "I used to be a vegetarian. I wouldn't have touched this on penalty of death." I coughed a little as I turned it over in my hands. "It's amazing."

Captain Summers frowned. "What?"

My eyes lifted to meet his. "How some things that I thought were so important really don't matter to me at all now." I bit down into the thick bread, the meat filling my mouth.

"Don't eat too quickly," he said. "You'll make yourself sick."

This brought on a fresh set of giggles. I had to put the food down and lower my head to the table to keep from toppling over with laughter. What was wrong with me tonight? Was it just that the weight I'd been living under for weeks, since the moment I'd woken with the sore throat back home, had finally lifted off me?

When I was able to raise my head again, I found Captain Summers smiling, his head cocked to the side as he watched me.

My eyes widened when I finally noticed he didn't have his mask on.

"You'll get sick," I said.

"Don't worry about it."

"I'm not," I said, although that wasn't the exact truth. I knew myself enough by now to recognized *that* at least. "But I am still sick. I'm probably still contagious."

He sighed. "Yeah, but I just can't stand wearing it anymore."

The frustration in his voice surprised me. So he was as sick of this entire situation as the rest of us were.

He glanced up at me. "I want it to be over." He suddenly pushed his chair back and stood, grabbing his keys from the table. "I'll be back in the morning," he said.

"Wait," I found myself saying. I had to say something, right? He had helped me, once again. I brought his name to my tongue for the first time. "David, I…"

He turned to me then, and I saw a veil of sadness descending over his features. It hardened until he was the person I'd seen the morning of my first roll call. Someone I couldn't touch.

"Don't," he said, lifting a hand. "I'm not the one to thank. Not at all."

And he was gone.

* * * *

A knock on the door woke me up, almost sending me tumbling off the couch into what would have been a painful land on my injured arm.

Someone moved across the room. David. No, it was Captain Summers.

I rolled my eyes at myself. Whatever. It was too early to pry my feelings apart to know what to call him.

Besides, he was glancing my way and motioning for me to sit up, which I did with about as much grace as a beached whale.

With one hand he placed the clear mask over his nose and mouth while he grabbed the doorknob with the other.

"Sergeant," he said, taking a step back.

A man walked into the room. He was in a darker uniform than David, with a clear mask that covered his entire face, and he even had his military cap still on.

"Captain Summers." The man's thick neck, the kind only chronic weight-lifters had, turned as he took in the room. His eyes landed on me for a second, then came back to David.

"I received some news last night. About a girl who survived the disease's last stage." He nodded in my direction. "I assume this is she."

"Sergeant, yes, I—"

"What I don't understand is why I had to hear this from one of your subordinates and not directly from you. I flew in this morning to see what the reality of the situation was."

"Sir, I wanted to make sure the girl really did make it through the night before alerting you."

David looked as calm as ever, but I thought I heard the slightest edge to his voice.

The Sergeant's eyebrows went up. "And for that you had to bring her to your private quarters?"

"I thought it was the safest place."

"Yes, I'm sure." The Sergeant's eyes travelled over me, making me want to wrap my arms around my body. "She looks stable enough, now. I'll have some guards take her to the testing wing."

My eyes widened.

"The testing wing, sir?" David said.

"We need to know why she survived."

"That's easy," I said.

The Sergeant turned to me as if he'd heard a piece of furniture speak. "Be quiet," he hissed.

Next to him, David shook his head gently.

Well, I wasn't about to let them drag me off to be tested that easily. I was preparing to leap (or more likely wobble) to my feet, when David's voice stopped me.

"Sir, I've been thinking of delaying sending her to the testing wing, just for another week. I would like her to look presentable when the cameras get here next Monday."

The Sergeant turned back to him. "Why?"

"Well, with your permission, sir, I would like to have her speak to the public. She is, after all, the only success story we have."

I held my breath. Could he have been planning this since last night? To use me to his advantage?

"The public needs to see her," he continued. "If they see that she came here and got better, then they'll quiet down again and allow us to do our jobs."

The Sergeant watched him for a few seconds, his whole body tense with whatever thoughts were running through his head. David, however, had the same calm, indifferent look he usually had.

"Very well," the Sergeant finally said. "Get her ready for Monday and after she's been interviewed, send her to be tested."

"Yes, sir."

With one more look in my direction, the older man turned around and left.

David exhaled as soon as the door closed. He turned to me and frowned. "What?"

"So you're just going to use me to say whatever you want to the people out there." I couldn't keep the anger out of my voice.

He blinked a few times. "Are you seriously angry at me for keeping you from being tested on?"

"Oh, sure, because that's all it was. It couldn't possibly be that you need me to say these things to keep the centers you thought up from looking like the failure they are." I knew what I was saying could get me a bullet through the forehead. I could even see his gun. But I had to say them; I couldn't keep letting him toy with me.

David stood very still. When he spoke, his voice was almost inaudible. "I know how wrong I was, Maya. But I'm not using you to clear my name. If I could tear these places down, I would." He shrugged. "You don't have to believe me. I'm not sure I would either if I were in your position. But, at least until next week, I can keep you safe."

I snorted. Was that supposed to make me feel better? I'd just survived a very bad scenario of death-by-fingernails and been thrown right into another. "And afterwards?"

"I'll think of something else."

I shook my head. "It's not very comforting."

"It's all I've got."

Chapter Twenty

David set a room up for me in front of his.

"No, I want to go back to the main hall."

He shook his head. "You can't be around so many sick people."

"Then bring Tom and Jessica here."

"They're sick as well."

"I don't care. Now that we know how to stop the disease from killing us, it shouldn't matter if they're sick."

David sighed. "Maya, we don't really know if just holding you down saved you. It could have been many other factors. I've actually heard of cases where the person still died despite being restrained. Their hearts just gave out. There's something else that allowed you to survive."

"Oh, so you're all for the doctors turning me into a science experiment?"

He rolled his eyes, a gesture I'd never imagined he would do. For a second I caught sight of the sixteen year old boy he must have been just a few years ago. My stomach knotted just a bit, warmth filling my body. I hated myself for welcoming the sensation.

Despite the worries about next week, I took the time that first day to enjoy how well I was starting to feel. Even after only hours since the violent Tearing attack, my body was starting to pull itself back together. I still coughed every once in a while, but the pain was gone, as if it'd ruptured within me and disappeared. I hadn't felt this comfortable in my own body in weeks.

Of course, I still had no idea what David's real intentions were with the whole interview deal and that bugged me, but for now, I saw no option but to go along with his plan.

He did, however, do as I asked and brought my friends to my room when night fell.

Jessica squeaked when she saw me and lunged at me, her arms choking most of the air out of my chest. I smiled, though I felt the tight rattling in her chest that let me know the coughing spasms had already started for her.

I was about to hug Tom when David handed me a mask. "Put it on."

"I've drunk from their same bowls and cups; I've shared blankets with them for weeks. There's no way I'm putting that on."

David threw his arms up and left the room, trailing frustration behind him.

When I turned back to my friends, I saw the bright surprise on their faces. "What's the matter?"

"You're going to get killed if you keep talking to him like that," said Tom.

I looked away. "We have an arrangement of sorts."

"Which is what?"

"Well, you two will be staying here with me for now."

"Really?" Jessica said. She looked around the room which, though not plush or even too big, provided three cots and a bathroom of our own.

"Yes."

Tom frowned. "What is he getting out of it?"

"I've promised to speak in front of the cameras next week."

"And say what?"

"I don't know. I guess say something about Levelry, how it helped me get better, how great it is. That kind of stuff."

"So you're going to do it?" Jessica asked.

"I have to." I told them everything that had happened this morning, hoping they'd give me some new perspective on the whole thing.

Tom's eyes stayed on me as I spoke of David, the slightest of creases growing on his forehead.

"But then they'll take you to be tested," Jessica said. She looked on the verge of a crying spell. I reached out and grabbed her hand. It was too hot.

"Lay down, Jessica. Someone will bring us food and since we have our own lights in here, we don't have a curfew." For some reason, being able to turn lights on and off at will had been the room's most exciting feature for me when I'd first stepped inside. Pretty pathetic, to be thrilled about something so simple.

Tom and I helped her shaky body to the nearest cot, luxuriously set up with sheets, a thick blanket, and a pillow. Just looking at it made me sleepy.

"You should have seen Elize's face when we told her you were still alive," Jessica said when I'd brought the blanket up to her chin. Her eyes were already half-closed.

It was so ridiculous that someone who was in the later stages of the Tearings, as Elize was, should feel affronted that another sufferer had actually survived. Shouldn't it have given her hope? But her anger was deeper than logic could reach.

I watched as Jessica fell asleep, curling up into a ball beneath the blanket. Despite its thickness, she still shivered.

Tom walked to his own cot. "I heard her coughing a lot this morning." He grabbed the blanket off it.

"When we start hearing it more often, then we have to keep an eye on her. I doubt anyone besides us will help her."

Tom placed his blanket over Jessica's body. His shoulder pressed against me, a comforting weight.

"And you, are you sick?" I asked.

He hesitated.

"Tom."

"I had a sore throat this morning. It's not as bad now."

I reached out and took his hand in mine, squeezing it in reassurance.

He was silent for a bit, but from the lines on his face I could tell there was something he wanted to say.

Finally he turned to me. "You need to do whatever they want. Anything that will keep you out of the testing wing. If you go in there…"

"I know."

"Do you think that guy, Captain Summers, will really help you after next week?"

Did I? If I gave him what they wanted, would there be any need to keep me safe? My head screamed that I'd be locked up seconds after the interview. But a flash of David's face filled my mind, his eyes watching me, unguarded. His words last night, kind and careful. Intimate. What did it all mean?

I had the sudden need to see him.

"You're smiling," Tom said. He sounded as confused as I felt.

I turned away. "Yes, I think he'll help me."

And at that moment, I really believed it.

* * * *

The next couple of days passed quickly, with Tom and Jessica led down each morning for roll call, then brought back up before dinner.

I wasn't allowed to leave the floor where our room was, though. Every day I headed to David's office which was a few doors down and sat to wait for any letters to type. The first day there were two rather short ones, the second day only one. And today, there'd been nothing on my desk when I got there.

David sat with his elbows on the desk, pretending to read the same piece of paper that had been sitting in front of him for the past three days.

After sitting still for half an hour, I stood.

He turned to me. "What the matter?"

"Do you have anything to read at least? I can't sit doing nothing all day."

He leaned away from the desk so he could open one of the drawers. I walked closer, coming to where he sat. The open drawer held mounds of papers, paperclips, and even post-its. It looked like any desk anywhere else. At the bottom of the mess, though, was a book.

"*The Brothers Karamazov*," I read. "Never got to that one."

David lifted it out and handed it to me. "I started it a while ago and never got a chance to finish it." He looked up at me. "Maybe you can tell me how it ends."

"Yes." I pushed away the thought that I might not get a chance to finish it, either, if I ended up as a guinea pig.

I was turning the book over to read the back when a piece of paper fell to the floor. No, it was a piece of cardboard.

I bent down and picked it up before David could.

Turning it over, the cardboard came to life with color. Yellows and greens lifted off the dull surface, bringing a dandelion to full bloom.

The small painting was so delicate I thought it'd disintegrate in my hands. As I looked, I caught a tiny pencil line etched on the side. It only had one word: Tatiana.

David reached out and took it gently from my hands.

"My sister did it." His eyes traveled along the painting. "I haven't looked at it in months, with…" he gestured to the room around us, "all of this going on."

"It's beautiful. She's a wonderful artist."

His eyes never leaving the image, he nodded. "She was."

Damn. I swallowed. "I'm sorry."

David had a thin veil of a smile on his lips. "We had an entire room full of her paintings. She was putting together a portfolio for a gallery when she got sick."

I opened my mouth to say something, anything, but he looked so lost in what he was seeing inside his head that I closed it again.

"Some of the centers were already up and running by then, but since I had a title, practically handed to me because of who I am, I was able to keep her home."

"Wait, what do you mean because of who you are?"

He finally looked up from the painting. "My dad was an army General. Decorated with countless metals for all sorts of heroic things. The only reason my superiors made me Captain was because I was his son. It was also why they listened to me at all when I came up with the basic idea for the healing centers." He scoffed, shaking his head. "But at least my title was able to save her from this place." He sighed. "This was the last thing she painted in the safe house where I was hiding her after my father died. I actually asked her, trying to tease a smile from her on one of the last days, why she'd chosen such a common thing to paint. A weed. She told me that she'd been watching it for days and that despite the weather, the birds that pecked at it, the sun that scorched it, that weed survived." His voice shook when he said the last word.

I didn't know what to do. My impulse was to touch him, to comfort him the same way I would like to be comforted, but how would he take it?

His hand rose halfway, hesitating for a beat on its way to me. Without allowing myself to think about it, I clasped it in mine.

His voice was an urgent whisper. "Maya, I never meant for this place to be the way it is. I wanted to provide the people who were sick with care, with whatever hope I could give them for finding a cure. But after the preliminary ideas, and after my father died, I wasn't allowed to demand changes or to speak out against everything that was so wrong. In their eyes, without my dad to back me up, I'm just any other inexperienced twenty-two year old."

Behind the coolness and the façade of power, he was really that young?

"The only thing I could do was threaten them with bringing in reporters. That was the only thing that allowed me to make some changes, like the blankets and the food. But I don't know how long even that will continue. I hate what the government has done and what they'll continue to do, but I don't know how to fix it. All I can do is watch it happen and hope I can help a few people."

"That's not enough," I whispered.

"No. I know it's not." His hand twitched in mine.

And there, watching David wrestle with a guilt that was tearing him up as much as the disease did to its sufferers, was when the idea got loose in my head.

* * * *

I didn't mention anything to Tom or Jessica about what I was planning on doing. I figured they'd try to talk me out of it, so there was no point. Besides, now that Jessica was nearing the last days of the disease and Tom himself was struggling through fever spells, they both had more than enough to worry about.

I said nothing to David, either.

He kept assuring me he'd find a way to stop them from taking me to the testing wing, but, by the dark patches under his eyes that grew as the days passed, I knew he hadn't found a real answer yet.

So the rest of the week passed, the hours tight with tension, and Monday finally came.

With it arrived the camera crew.

A guard burst into the room I shared with Jessica and Tom, followed by a woman wearing so much makeup everyone could probably have seen her every eye movement from across the building. I could even see bright lipstick peeking out from behind the thin black mask that covered her nose and mouth.

"You two," the guard said, pointing to Tom and Jessica, "head downstairs."

"You're Maya?" the woman asked, placing a large silver box on the floor.

"Yes."

"I'm Alba." She extended her hand then thought better of it. "I'll be making sure you are presentable today. Okay, I need you to take a shower and use these," she said, handing me two purple bottles. Shampoo and conditioner, the fancy kind hair salons used. She pulled out a bottle of body wash, and a razor, which she handed over without hesitation. Wasn't she scared I might try to attack her?

But I did as she said, sighing under the fresh, sweet scent of the products. If I closed my eyes and tried not to think, I could almost imagine I was at home, relaxing after swim practice.

I had just stepped out of the shower when Alba opened the door.

"Jesus!" I said, grabbing the towel next to me.

She paid no attention to my frowns and unwillingness to stand naked in front of her and just handed me a pair of dark brown linen pants and a soft, cream-colored cotton shirt.

"Get out and I'll put the clothes on," I said.

"Don't be ridiculous—"

"Out." I would not be bullied into this. I might not have much left that was mine, but my body certainly was.

When I was dressed, I had to sit and endure all kinds of preening that set my teeth on edge. Had I really spent time in front of a mirror applying foundation and powder, eye-shadow, and lip gloss? Had I really wasted time out of my day for that? It seemed ridiculous now.

Finally, Alba stepped back and smiled. "You're done."

"Oh, thank God," I muttered.

"Don't you want to look at yourself?"

"Not really."

"Oh, come on." She ushered me to my feet and put a large hand mirror in front of me. I looked at myself. Or who I thought was me.

It was incredible, really. She'd erased the disease's marks from me, smoothing out my thin skin and adding color to make me look not like someone who'd missed death by a breath but someone with bucketfuls of health. Even my hair, an untamed, short mess until last night, was brushed in such a way that made it seem fashionable.

I could only stare. Well, whatever happened, at least I'd look presentable for Derek, if he was still healthy and watching, and not in a center himself. I felt a twinge. I'd probably never see Derek again, and I'd been so awful to him. I wanted to tell him how he, or his image, helped me in the isolation room. To apologize for the horrible way I'd treated him, to thank him for making Mom happy.

"It's good, isn't it?" Alba said.

Tears threatened to roll down my perfectly powdered face. I blinked them away. She would probably have a heart attack if I messed up her work. "Yeah."

The door opened behind us and a guard entered the room. "Let's go," he said.

I gave silent thanks that I didn't have a cough anymore, because the way we hurried down the many corridors would have propelled me into a major spasm. Actually, I realized, I felt close to normal. How long would that last?

We walked right by the main hall but did not enter it. Even from the quick glance, though, I could see how much they'd changed it. There were tables now, and chairs, though no beds. They'd probably set up another room as the "bedrooms" or whatever.

Two guards led Alba away to who knew where, then shoved me into a space that had been set up as a sitting room of sorts, with two large sofas in a thick, shiny velvet that looked like the kind used to make Halloween costumes. Whoever had picked the furniture out had not had the best taste.

"Sit."

I picked a sofa and did as I was told.

My heart was beating too quickly. Nerves made my hands so shaky I had to clasp them together to keep them still. Slowly, I breathed in and out, like I used to do before swim matches. I smiled as the nerves loosened their hold a bit.

The door opened.

David stepped in and my heart pounded again.

He paused by the door, watching me. For a minute, I couldn't think what had him so captivated, then I remembered I didn't look like I'd been living under a bridge anymore.

He, on the other hand, despite his resplendent uniform, looked worse than I'd ever seen him.

"Have you slept at all?" I whispered.

He waved my words away and stepped closer, lifting a piece of paper for me to see. "Maya, this has the questions the reporter is going to ask you, followed by the…appropriate answers." He flicked his eyes to me. "Read them over. You have about forty-five minutes before they get here. Since it's live, there are no do-overs. Do you understand?" His gaze dug into me.

"Yes." I understood it too well.

"Just say what's on the page and you'll be fine."

I glanced over the words. "They could have given it to me a couple of days ago, not minutes before I'm on air."

David rubbed his forehead with a hand almost as unsteady as mine was. "You don't have to give the answers word for word. Just the basic idea." He kept watching me, as if he sensed something was off.

I looked away. "Are Tom and Jessica okay?"

"I saw them a few minutes ago. She was coughing too much to have her in the room while they film, so the Sergeant separated her. Tom is still in the main hall."

"That's not good. What if she starts tearing at her skin? She needs Tom to keep an eye on her." My voice had an edge of panic I didn't like, but I couldn't help it. If I was going to do this, then I needed to know my friends were all right.

"I'll check on her every few minutes. She'll be okay."

I swallowed. "Can I talk to Tom?"

David shook his head. "No, he's already positioned for when the show starts."

"Show?" I smiled.

"It is a performance, isn't it?"

He held my gaze, meeting my smile with his own faint one.

"I'll go check on Jessica and you, read those answers."

"Aye, aye, Captain." I made a vague salute, and was rewarded with one of David's sharp smiles. I hoped I'd see him one more time. But I doubted it.

Once he left, I slumped back on the sofa and brought the paper up so I could read it. Okay.

Let's do this.

* * * *

"Good afternoon, everyone, I am Caroline Jackson of Channel Four News. My crew and I have the privilege of being the first news team allowed in Levelry Health Center. As many of you are aware, this and many other centers cater solely to the victims of the new flu epidemic, the one that's being called the Tearings.

"We have just seen how wonderful this place looks, and now, right here, we'll get a chance to speak with one of the many success stories."

She smiled widely through her clear mask, waiting a beat while her words caused the supposed amount of flurry in the viewers. My eyes looked around the room, at the three cameras, the three men manning them covered in protective wear, and the two guards standing by the door.

Slowly, I felt one of the cameras turn its eye towards me. I had to keep myself from squirming beneath the weight of the millions of people watching me through it.

"With us, we have seventeen-year-old Maya Salaise, who, if it hadn't been for this center, would already be dead. Instead, she appears before us restored completely back to health."

I could almost hear the gasps rounding the country as this settled in the viewers' heads. Did they believe it?

The newswoman, Caroline, turned her large smile towards me. "It's wonderful to see you looking so well, Maya," she said. Her voice sounded as if we'd known each other for years before this interview.

"Thank you, Caroline."

"Tell us a little about the center and about the treatment process offered here." She blinked, but her smile never moved.

I knew what I was supposed to say. The words shuffled through my head, ready to be spoken if I allowed it.

My mouth shifted into a smile as well. Those words disappeared, pushed aside by the ones that really needed to be said.

"Well, Caroline, that's a great question. Levelry is certainly special, though not in the way we were all led to believe." I paused. This was it. "The truth is that this place, like all the rest of the centers, is a death camp."

Caroline's smile wavered.

From the corner of my eye I saw the guards shifting. But we were on air, live. Unless the officials were willing to explain why I was cut off or removed from the screen, they'd have to allow me to explain. Even if they took the risk and removed me, stopping the interview would have the same effect on the viewers as my words would: it would create doubt.

So I continued. "The government wants you to believe that the people suffering from this illness are being provided with the best medical care available, when the reality is that everyone here is dying from starvation, from lack of the very basics like hygiene and blankets. I, and the rest of the ill, are locked in these centers, unable to communicate with the outside world and living under the threat of being shot by one of the many guards who roam this place. Like these," I said, pointing to the two guards by the door. The camera followed my finger, catching the uniforms and, most importantly, the rifles.

"These people abuse us, using the power handed to them by the government. But that's not the worst of it. Many of the ill people that come to the centers are taken to what the officials call the 'testing wing'. The building, in fact, could be better called a torture chamber. Think of the experiments that have been done to animals. That's what they are doing to your loved ones." Tom's face passed through my mind, his smile. "They say it's to find a cure, but it's inhumane what goes on behind those walls.

"And you see me, yes, I am better, almost cured completely, but it hasn't been from anything Levelry has done for me."

The door opened and the Sergeant charged in, motioning for the cameras to stop filming. The three men looked at the newswoman, who seemed to be listening to her earpiece.

"Don't let them fool you—" I said.

"That's all the time we have for this afternoon," Caroline said. The cameras shifted away from me as the guards charged forward and yanked me to my feet.

"You can help!" I screamed. "You can all—"

Something hard slapped the side of my face. I tasted blood.

"Lock her up," the Sergeant hissed next to me.

The guards started pulling at me again, but I wasn't going to give up that quickly. I jabbed my elbows into everything I could touch, kicking out with my feet. I shrieked as loudly as I could, hoping to get some of it recorded, though I assumed by now the crew had been ordered to stop filming. It didn't matter. The damage was done.

It took four guards to drag me to another room and bolt me inside. As soon as they released me, I lunged forward, ready to rip into anything I could grab. I managed to dig my nails into someone's face, but with the crash of a rifle against my still injured arm, I had to let go.

The door slammed closed and bolted.

I threw myself against it. Somewhere in the back of my head I knew I couldn't open it, not even by force, but my body was reacting solely to the rage coursing through it as violently as the disease had done just days before.

I didn't stop until my hands had gashes from beating at the door and walls with such force. It might have been only minutes since the interview had ended, but it felt like I'd always been stuck in that room. Like I'd been born there, so full of anger I was shaking.

Panting, I sat down. I had to calm down to be able to think properly.

The room was bare, with only one naked light-bulb throwing harsh light at the walls, and no windows. So there was no chance of escape. I hadn't really been counting on it.

I leaned back against the wall and forced myself to slow my breathing. This was not the time to pass out.

So many thoughts flitted around in my head. Had Derek seen it? Had people understood what I'd said? Had they heard the last few words? They had to have realized something was wrong, but the question was if they'd do anything about it or just continue on through their daily lives with blinders blocking the truth.

My breathing was almost back to normal when the door opened and David came in, yanking his mask off and flinging it across the room.

I leapt to my feet.

"Maya, what did you do?" His voice was tight with fear. He grabbed my hands, pulling me closer. "I can't help you now. I can't get you out of this one!" His fingers were painful against my skin, but I clutched at him with just as much force.

"I had to. It was my only chance to tell people the truth."

"They'll torture you!"

"I know. But they were going to do it anyway, right?" My hands shook in his as the words really reached me.

David felt it. His arms wrapped around me, enveloping me in his warmth as I started to shake. I pressed my head against his chest and listened to the rapid pounding beneath. One of his hands gripped my short hair.

"Do you think they'll take me away?" I whispered through chattering teeth.

"I don't know. I don't know anything."

He turned his head and kissed my hair. Gently, he lifted his head so that we were face to face. His dark eyes were no longer the blank mirrors they'd been when I'd met him. They glittered.

I brushed his cheek with my hand, feeling the strength, the intelligence beneath my fingers, knowing that I'd most likely never have another chance to be with him like this.

I leaned in and brought my lips to his.

David was still for an instant, as if I'd taken him by surprise. Suddenly, his grip tightened on me, pulling me in as close as I could get. His taste filled my mouth, sweet and sharp at the same time. His hand pressed against my back, sending shivers down my spine as I clutched at his uniform, wanting to feel the skin underneath.

With a groan, he pulled away from me.

I gasped as I heard the footsteps nearing the room.

"I'll find a way to get you out," he whispered, his eyes burning in front of me. "I'll find one."

"Tom and Jessica," I said.

"I'll do what I can."

I nodded and released him.

In seconds, the room was full of guards.

Chapter Twenty-One

They took me to the building next to the crops. The window Tom had seen me through blinked at me as the guards pulled me in through the doors.

By then, I'd stopped fighting. There was no point, and it'd probably be a better idea to save my energy for whatever was coming next.

I was, at least, relieved I wasn't forced into a truck or another bus to be taken anywhere else. One horror avoided.

They pulled me past the collection of cells that Tom had mentioned, most of them empty despite the arrival of the last bus, and through a set of heavy metal doors into a back area.

"In there," one of the guards told the two that had hold of my arms.

"There" was an empty room with tiles on the floor. There was drain in the center. Didn't bode too well for whatever would happen in here. It smelled like ammonia and something darker beneath it.

Without a word, the guards left me in the foreboding room and bolted the door behind them. I sighed and sat down. Exhaustion was making it difficult to really muster up any kind of fear. I wished there was a window in the room, though. I didn't want to die in here without a single sliver of sunlight.

Who knew how long I'd be in here? They wouldn't just shoot me, not when I was the only one who'd survived the disease so far. No, they'd tear me apart looking for something that might end this pandemic. Maybe, despite everything, I could help someone out there at some point. I had to think that perhaps my death wouldn't just be a waste.

Tom and Jessica. Would they be all right? And David. His scent, his face, travelled through me. I shook my head. I couldn't think about him now.

An hour or so passed before the Sergeant finally appeared.

He walked into the room alone, despite much shifting from the guards behind him, and closed the door.

He watched me for a couple of minutes, a thin smile slicing his face.

"Very stupid what you pulled today," he finally said.

I shrugged. "I don't think so."

"Do you really think the people watching believed a single word? Do you think they thought you were anything more than a hysterical girl making up stories?"

"I think you underestimate the public."

He chuckled. "Really? They've been hearing rumors for months and no one has done a thing, not even bothered to ask a single question."

I shook my head. "I don't believe that. I'm sure whoever asked questions was punished for them."

"Well, it doesn't matter either way for you. You will not get out of this place alive. I can guarantee that."

I held his gaze. "I figured as much."

"And we'll be working diligently to get the interview off the air so that no one else can see it."

"It's too late."

"We'll see." He moved to the door. "Make yourself comfortable, Maya, you'll be here for a while."

* * * *

The doctor who came in with a tray of needles barely looked at me. I felt my stomach fall at the sight.

Needles. Again. I could stand the mild shocks of electricity and even the probing, but the needles...

The woman in the lab coat, someone who at some point had been a doctor ready to help, to cure sick people, grabbed my bruised arm, lifting the tunic out of the way.

I winced. The sores from the last injection still hurt.

"Hold still."

It was surprising to hear her voice at all. She, like the other doctor who was on the night shift, usually just came and went without a word. I supposed it helped them to avoid making any kind of contact with me that wasn't medical. It made it easier to do what they had to.

For the past few days (no idea how many they could have been), they'd taken blood from me, bits of my hair, nail clippings, and even a urine sample. They probably had no result back yet from whichever hellish lab was on their payroll, but they'd wasted no time in filling me with chemicals.

This was the fifth injection.

The doctor pushed the plunger down and the liquid, clear and thick, seeped in my body. The burning started at once.

I'd promised myself I wouldn't cry out this time, but it was impossible. The pain was almost as bad as the one the Tearings had caused.

At first, I couldn't understand why they needed to test me at all, but after the second injection, feeling pain so similar to the disease itself, I'd realized that they were filling me with a concentrated version of the Tearings that sent me straight to the last stage. They were probably hoping to create a vaccine using whatever antibodies, if any, I'd developed.

Before the first injection, they'd brought in a chair with straps on the armrests. They'd been trying me down with each round of testing, keeping me from harming myself. On cue, the guard waiting by the door stepped forward and helped the doctor tighten the straps.

I moaned as the pain spread through me. My back arched with it, forcing the straps into my arms, right into the sores I'd developed from the first few doses.

The doctor and guard just stared at me, waiting.

Minutes later, the burning ebbed, then stopped.

The doctor looked at her watch, nodded, and wrote something down. "It's less," she muttered.

I slumped forward, panting. Had the effects really lasted less this time? Whatever her watch said, the pain was endless when I was in the midst of it.

Nodding to no one, the doctor turned around and left the room. The guard undid the straps then followed her out.

I was left alone again, staring at the tiles and trying not to think of David, Tom, Jessica, mom, or Derek. I tried to empty my mind of everything that could hurt me.

That was what my life was reduced to, minutes of pain followed by nothing.

* * * *

A shriek woke me. At first I was convinced it was someone next to me, or in front of me, screaming wordlessly. But there was no one in the room.

I blinked to clear the last bits of sleep from my eyes.

A second later, a piercing red light flooded the room. I hadn't even noticed the black spot on the wall opposite me, a few feet above the door, from where the light was coming. It was an alarm of some sort.

The light held still for a few seconds, then blinked out. I held my breath and waited until it returned. On and off, on and off.

Footsteps rushed down the corridor and past my door.

The thundering boots were what really shook me completely awake. If the guards were running, whatever was happening was not just a practice test. It was real.

I leaned forward, testing my body. Nothing told me I'd not be able to stand up, but I had to take my time. If something major was happening, then I needed to be ready, for anything. If I had any chance of getting out of this room, I had to be ready to take it.

Slowly, I lifted myself up, clutching the chair as tightly as I could.

My legs were steadier than I'd expected and I was able to stand on my own in a matter of moments.

Just in time, too, because someone was trying to get into the room.

I looked around, but of course, there was nothing I could use as a weapon. If I'd been a bit stronger, I would have used the chair, at least, but as it was, I couldn't imagine holding it up for too long.

There was no more time, though. Whoever was behind that door was about to open it.

I leapt forward and pressed against the wall next to the door, hoping to at least surprise the person, and maybe craft an exit out of that.

The hinges groaned and the door opened.

In the red glare, I didn't recognize him that first instant, so I pushed right into him, slamming him into the opposite wall. My nails grabbed at any skin they could find.

"Maya!"

I gasped and released him.

"David."

He put a hand to his neck, where I'd grabbed him. There was a collection of half-moons all along his throat. He looked up, his eyebrows lifted in a mixture of emotions I couldn't tell apart.

"Come on, we only have a few minutes." He extended his hand.

This was not the time for hesitation. I either trusted him or I didn't.

I took his hand.

The hallway was filled with smoke, thickening the red light and making my eyes sting. "What is this?"

"Tear gas."

David rushed us down the hall as the gas started to pick at my lungs, nose, and eyes. I covered my mouth with my free hand, though it really did nothing to stop the gas. This was the only time I wished for one of the black masks.

David coughed. "It's not much farther."

We rounded a corner and almost ran straight into another guard. David shoved me backward before the other man could see me.

"Captain?" the guard said.

"What are you still doing up here? Didn't I order all of you to secure the prisoners?" His voice was a knife through the hall, cutting the noxious gas in two.

"Sir, I was told to check on the girl—"

"I've already checked on her. She's dead."

I could feel the doubt in the guard's silence.

David coughed again. "Go back to the main building. We need to find out who set this off." There was no room for further questions in his voice and the guard responded to it as he'd been trained to do.

"Yes, sir."

He ran down to the stairway.

We waited for a minute or two, feeling our eyes swell with the gas, then followed him down the hallway. But instead of turning to the stairs, David led us into a small room, more like a closet. He closed the door behind us.

A light-bulb's yellow glow coated us.

"Here, put these on," he said, handing me a pair of cotton jogging pants and a long sleeved black shirt.

I didn't hesitate, just took my tunic top and pants off. This was not the time for prudishness.

As I slipped the shirt over my head, David lifted one of my feet and stuffed it into a sneaker. "They're a bit big," he said.

"Just tie them really tightly." I was actually surprised at how closely he'd guessed my sizes.

"This," he said, handing me a pouch the texture of tent canvas, "is a waterproof and fire proof bag. Inside there's some money and a disposable cell phone. I don't know the number, I don't want to know it, but I've written mine on the inside of this bag, in the lining. Call me when you are safe."

I had to press against him to hear his voice over the blaring siren.

"Wait," I said. "Where are we going? What's the plan?"

"There's no time. We have to go, Maya."

He pulled the door open and we plunged once more into the gas, running down the stairs until we were on the first floor.

"Through the back," he said.

Together, we moved down a narrow passage to a boarded up door. It looked as rusty and old as the boards

I'd tried to remove in the main hall the night I found out Mom had died.

"We can't get through," I said.

"Yes, we can. Grab one end there." He motioned to the board's left side, while he gripped the right one.

"On three, pull with everything you have, okay?"

"Yeah."

"One…two…three!"

I bent my knees and pulled. In the moment it took the wood to move, I was already picturing our capture, being thrown back into the tiled room, seeing David dragged into a similar one.

But the board did give under our combined strength.

"Go!" David yelled and I ran out, into the night.

Fresh air filled my lungs, pushing out the gas.

The darkness was a comfort after the red light, but even from where we were, we could see the flames leaping high into the sky.

"What is that?"

"Levelry." David's face was bathed in the dancing glow. "The main building."

"But all the people!" I gasped. "Tom and Jessica!"

"They're safe, Maya. I made sure of that."

Had he done this on his own?

We heard crunching footsteps close to us, too close. David's eyes narrowed in concentration as he stood still, using the long shadow from a nearby tree to hide himself.

It was another guard, this one armed with everything he could hold.

David flicked his eyes to me, letting me know without words that I had to stay as quiet and still as possible.

The steps drew closer. David slipped a knife from his belt and leapt forward. The movement sent both him and the guard right into the dirt. Seeing who it was, the guard was too shocked to act. David buried the knife into his chest.

After everything I'd seen, it was ridiculous to gasp, but I couldn't stop myself. Someone else dead. Someone who was just following orders.

David's hand, slick with sweat but steady, took mine. "Let's go."

We left the body behind. Had he died already or was he struggling with his breath all alone?

The two of us lunged into the line of trees behind the crops as shouts rang out ahead of us.

"Damn," David said. His head turned right to left. "I think we're going to have to change plans a bit. If we continue this way we'll run straight into them."

I nodded. "What are the options now?"

"There's really only one. The river that runs in front of the center." He stood up straighter and peered out at the night, watching for movement. "It's deep, and the fence on the other side across is electrified, but there's a tunnel on the opposite bank, where an old drainage pipe used to run when this place was a factory, and when there used to be a building on the other side of the canal. If you can get through that tunnel, then you'll be across, near to the forest line on the other side. No one will be able to see you there. The thing is that the tunnel has been underwater for the past few months, so you'll have to swim through it."

"How long is it?"

"Ten feet, maybe twelve."

A flare popped into the sky, just feet from us. "We have to go, David."

His eyes, full of reflected fire, turned and caught mine. "Can you swim?"

I smiled. "Yeah, that I can do."

He nodded. "Okay."

We ran through the trees. Branches hit my face, scratching it with their needle thinness, but we couldn't stop. If we did, they'd catch us.

Just focus on your feet, I told myself. *Don't trip.*

My shoes tangled on roots only once, but I was able to grab on to a tree and pull myself up. David took my hand again, lending me his trained, sure footing. I stepped where he did, letting his rhythm guide my own.

We came to the edge of the forest, where the river sliced through it like a wound.

I looked down. It wasn't too far a jump into the dark water, but it was the farthest I'd ever dived.

David also looked down. He was panting, his pulse racing against my skin, but his eyes were focused. This must have been what he looked like as a soldier.

"The tunnel has to be there." He pointed to one side of the opposite bank. "It's covered up, but it's there."

I frowned. There was nothing there that I could see. "Are you sure?"

He bit his lip and narrowed his eyes as he searched again. His face suddenly cleared. "Yes. I remember that piece of limestone protruding from the side because it was hell trying to work around it. The tunnel can't be more than four or five feet to the right of it."

I opened my mouth again, but a gunshot stopped my words. There was no time left for doubts.

"Get out of here, David. Go before they see you." They would probably already suspect him when they realized I was gone, but if they saw him now, they'd shoot him for sure, Captain or not. I wanted him to come with me, but I knew it was impossible. Even if I could convinced him to do it, I doubted he would fit into the tunnel.

His arms wrapped around me in a tight, frantic embrace. His heart, beating as quickly as a bird's, pulsed against mine.

"Swim hard," he whispered.

I nodded, stitching the words onto my very limbs.

Forcing myself away from him, I took one more look at the water beneath me. There was a slight current but it didn't look too powerful. If I could handle the ocean without problem, this shouldn't be too hard.

I tied the bag with the cell phone and money around one of the pants' belt loops then walked to the forest floor's edge.

"David." I closed my eyes in the darkness. "Thank you."

Taking a deep breath, I plunged into the river.

V.C. REPETTO

Chapter Twenty-Two

I hit the water as I'd done a million times before, my body sliding right in, my muscles adjusting to the element.

Kicking up, I propelled my head above the surface. The water's chill seeped into me in an instant, sending my teeth chattering. I turned around in a circle, getting my bearings. David was still by the edge, looking for me.

I lifted my arm and jerked it to the side, signaling that I was all right and for him to leave at the same time.

Shouts cut through the night, way too close to where David was standing. "Go!" I hissed. Another gunshot finally forced him away, leaving me alone in the shifting river.

There was no time to waste now; I had to find the tunnel's opening before any of the guards saw me. If they started shooting here, into the water, there was no chance I'd make it out alive.

I locked my eyes on the protruding limestone David had pointed out and swam close to the bank's wall, gripping its slippery edge. I needed to find the tunnel, because I didn't think I could climb back up.

My hands started feeling for the opening beneath the chilly water. Taking a deep breath, I dipped down and opened my eyes wide. I could barely see anything, though, just shifting darkness everywhere I turned.

Something brushed by my leg, making it twitch. Great. *Let it be leaves, just let it be leaves.*

I kicked whatever it was away and forced myself to focus. I'd have to go back up for more air soon, but I didn't have much more time to find the tunnel.

There was a slight difference in the water to my left. My hands felt it first, a little wave of movement that meant there was a change in the current.

There it was! I could make out a patch of darker water. That was the tunnel's opening. I ran my hands over it, feeling for the edges.

The metal tube wasn't much wider than I was, but I could probably swim through it without too much trouble.

I kicked back up to the surface and breathed through my nose, keeping my chin and mouth submerged so there'd be less of me to spot if anyone looked down.

The best, the fastest, option would be to swim with my hands at my sides, using just my legs, letting the water slide over me. But it was too dark in there to swim blindly. I wouldn't even be able to tell where the tunnel turned or ended. No, better to keep my arms out in front of me, even if it slowed me down a bit. It was only twelve feet long at most, right? I could make that, even with the shoes and clothes bogged down by water.

The voices were almost on me now. No more time to waste.

I exhaled a few times, pushing as much air as I could out of my lungs so that when I did take a deep breath, I could take in all my lungs could hold.

When I felt my body vibrating with energy, I sucked in and plunged down again.

I guided myself inside the tunnel, feeling the metal's slickness surrounding me. My legs kicked and I moved forward until I felt the river's open water replaced by a sense of tightness and an absolute darkness.

I swam like that, blind, for seconds, expecting to hit a wall, a rock, anything, at any moment. The only sound was the occasional thump of the bag attached to my pants hitting the tube.

Finally, my hands touched metal in front of me. I tapped the tube around me until I felt the opening again, right above me. The tunnel headed up now, meaning I was almost out. Good thing, too, since I didn't have much air left.

I kicked harder, using the tube's bottom to propel myself up, and smashed my hand against something hard.

A chill ran through me.

There was something blocking the way. A bubble of air escaped my mouth as I realized just how much trouble I was in.

I couldn't go back. I didn't have enough air to back up then turn around and swim all the way out of the tunnel. If I couldn't move whatever was blocking the way in the next few seconds, then it was game over.

I pressed both hands against the surface blocking the way and pushed. It didn't move.

Panic, so bright and loud it was impossible to ignore, was waiting to take over.

To have gone through all these weeks, through the Tearings, to drown. To die in *my* element, the one that felt like a second skin to me.

No. I wouldn't allow it.

I placed my feet on both sides of the tube, giving a thanks that I hadn't taken my shoes off, bent my knees, and propped myself up. I ignored the pressure in my chest that was as much a warning as the red light had been minutes ago.

My hands firmly planted against the stone or whatever blocked the way. I pushed, using my propped up legs for extra strength.

I closed my eyes and willed it to move.

A beat passed, then another. I almost gasped when I felt the object under my hands shift. It slid up with a shriek of concrete on metal. I pushed it to the side and lifted my head up through the opening.

Air.

I gulped it in, coughing, allowing myself a moment of relief. I was still alive.

Shouts reached me from across the river. I looked up and took in my surroundings. The tree line was still far from where I was and there was nothing else around me to hide behind. I had to reach the forest.

I pushed the block of cement, which had probably been placed over the hole to keep people from falling in, all the way out. I then eased the rest of my body out of the water. I flattened myself against the ground, hoping the night would hide me from the flashlights and from the still burning fire that moved on the opposite bank. From the amount of noise behind me, they'd probably already discovered I was gone.

Would all of Levelry burn to the ground? Had they already called for help?

If fire trucks came maybe I could...

But that thought crumbled as soon as I had it. If they saw the numbers tattooed on my arm, they'd take me right back to the center.

I crawled forward, stones pushing into my skin, as the noise increased. I didn't allow myself to look behind me.

But it wasn't only the guards who were chasing me. Thoughts did an even better job of it.

Mom. She'd died in there and I hadn't been able to do anything. Tom and Jessica, David, I was leaving all of them to their fates, saving myself. What kind of person did that?

A light brushed my clothes. They were checking the riverbank and the water.

I started moving again. I couldn't stop now, regardless of the guilt I felt. It was too late to turn back.

Keeping my head down, I crawled for what felt like hours. But finally the ground beneath me changed, filling with roots. I waited until I reached a large branch that bowed towards the ground and provided a bit of shadow, then stood up and moved deeper into the forest.

When I was pretty confident they wouldn't be able to see me from across the river, I broke into a run, not bothering to be quiet or subtle. All I needed was to get distance between me and Levelry.

There was only a dim moonlight lighting my way, so I tripped over and over, but I always got back up. My lungs seemed to expand as I ran and for the first time in a long time I felt like myself again. A body in powerful motion. Someone strong.

I heard the road before I saw it. Even this late, there were cars driving by. I stopped running when I could see the ribbon of cement that marked the way back to freedom.

Panting, I slid down a tree's trunk to the leaf-covered floor and sat until my heart slowed down a bit. My wet clothes clung to me in the night air, making me shiver.

I grabbed the bag that still hung from my belt and opened it. The bag had done its job and kept everything inside it dry. I brought out the cell phone but hesitated in turning it on. Probably not the best idea to use it now, not when the search was still on. For all I knew, David might already be paying for what he'd done for me.

As I placed the phone back, I checked the bundle of money. A few hundred dollars. Then, at the bag's very bottom, I touched something else.

I brought it out.

It was Tatiana's painting, the one of the dandelion. I couldn't see all of its colors in the darkness, but I knew they were there, the whites and yellows and greens, all waiting for daylight.

Why had David given me this? Was it just to remind me of him?

Carefully (although if the painting had survived this long it was practically as indestructible as the dandelion on it), I placed it back in the bag. I found myself smiling at the knowledge that it was with me, as if just having it shielded me.

I sat and watched the road. I waited to see dark buses or government vehicles of some sort, but all the cars I saw were regular ones, driven by people who had no idea, not even a glimmer, of what was happening just a few miles away.

I had two options now: stay in the forest and follow the road until I reached a gas station or bus stop, or try to get a ride.

Hitchhiking wasn't my idea of safety, but what waited behind me was even worse.

It was the dawn that finally forced me to decide. In the daylight, the search would expand and I'd surely be found.

I stood, my chilled muscles complaining at the sudden movement, and headed down to the road. I felt naked out in the open, without trees or darkness to hide me, but I stood still and tried to look as normal as possible. No one wanted a terrified girl in their car.

It didn't take too long to see headlights glowing nearer. I held my breath, expecting to see an ambulance ready to take me back.

But no, it was a smaller vehicle, a car, bruised and battered but rumbling with life.

I waved with my right arm, making sure the tattoo on the other one was hidden, and made myself smile.

I saw the driver hesitate. Normal, really, since I couldn't begin to imagine what I must have looked like. At the last minute, as the car was about to pass me, it swerved to the curb.

There was a woman behind the wheel. She didn't lower the window or open the door.

"I'm not sick," I called out.

She watched me, taking in my still wet clothes, my empty hands. After a second, she shrugged.

"I am," she said.

I blinked, suddenly noticing the slightly flushed cheeks, the shine in her eyes. "It's fine; I don't care."

The woman frowned. "Are you sure?"

"Yeah."

She gave me a small nod and opened the passenger side door.

I slid in. The car's heater was on pretty high, doing what it could to fight back the fever she was going through. I sighed with pleasure.

"I don't know how far I can take you," she said.

"It's all right. Anywhere is better than here."

She eased back onto the road.

"You really don't care that I'm sick?"

I shook my head. "Not really." I took a deep breath. "There are worse things."

"Are there?"

I nodded. "Yeah."

"Well, I'm Katrina."

"Maya."

She drove in silence. She didn't ask me why I was alone with nothing but a small bag, and I didn't ask her why she wasn't in an ambulance being taken to one of the centers.

I tried to sleep as the miles passed, but my mind wouldn't stay still, picking at wounds, bringing forward the faces of people I loved.

I'd left them behind.

Over and over my mind threw the words back at me.

I'd left them behind. And I probably wouldn't see them again. Would David even be able to answer the phone when I called?

I looked out the window at the sun's slow simmer to full power. Where would I be when it set this afternoon? The only thing I knew was that I wouldn't be with those I loved.

To stop this self-inflicted torture, I pulled my bag open and brought out Tatiana's painting again. It really was remarkable; each petal, each bit of pollen glowing with life.

"That's pretty," Katrina said. "Did you do it?"

"No. A friend gave it to me."

"What does it say on the back?"

On the back? Frowning, I turned the painting over.

There was just one word written in pen on the cardboard.

"Survive."

Tears gathered in my eyes as the knowledge that that was exactly what I had to do made its way into my heart.

For Tom, Jessica, Lesley, Sophia. For Mom and David. And even for Tatiana.

I had to survive.

The End

www.vcrepetto.wix.com/vcrepetto

Evernight Teen

www.evernightteen.com

6001623R00163

Made in the USA
San Bernardino, CA
28 November 2013